SECRET

BETROTHED #9

PENELOPE SKY

Hartwick Publishing

Secret

Copyright © 2020 by Penelope Sky

All rights reserved.

CONTENTS

ONE
CATALINA

WHEN HEATH HUNG UP ON ME, I DIDN'T TRY TO CALL back.

I didn't know what to feel. I was relieved that I'd called Heath before it was too late, that his heart was still beating when he took my call, that he was still the strong man who looked into my eyes as if there'd never been anyone else.

But I hated myself for what I did to Damien.

My own fucking brother.

I betrayed him. I betrayed my family.

For what, exactly? For sex? For some man I vowed never to love?

I sat against the headboard with my knees to my chest, the phone beside me, the screen dark. I was too nervous to turn on the TV or open my device to read. I chose to sit in the dark and wait for any subtle sound in the hope he would approach my door any moment...safe and sound.

Then I heard it, distant and faint, the heavy footsteps of a man coming down the hallway. The only reason I noticed was because I listened for it, waited to hear the sound. There was no one else awake at this time of night, so there wasn't any noise from my neighbors, no cars passing on the street outside my window.

Maybe my mind was playing tricks on me, but I jumped out of bed and headed to the front door anyway. I unlocked all the bolts and swung the door open, hoping to see that man on my doorstep.

And he was.

He took the last few steps to my doorway, his blue eyes focused on mine, not blinking, not sharing a single thought. He didn't seem angry, happy, anything. He was just...cold.

I was so happy to see him that tears formed in my eyes. But I had to ask something first. "Is Damien okay?"

He cocked his head slightly, as if the question offended him, as if he was annoyed I felt I had to ask at all. "Yes."

"Thank god." I stepped into his chest and wrapped my arms around him, my cheek moving to his heartbeat so I could feel it thump against my body. My ears could listen to it beat, listen to the way it was so slow and steady.

His hand slipped into my hair while his arm wrapped around my waist. He backed me into the apartment so we wouldn't be in the hallway any longer. His foot kicked the door shut behind him. He held me tight in front of the door, his fingertips lightly playing with my hair as I continued to grab on to him, to feel my aching heart start to heal now that he was there in the flesh. That was the hardest decision I'd ever had to make, and now that I was deliriously relieved by his return, I realized I had made the right one.

"Let's go to bed," he whispered into my hairline before he released me. It was almost five in the morning, so he was probably tired after the long day and night he just had. His fingertips slid down my cheek before they finally broke contact.

Then I was cold.

He entered my bedroom and got undressed. His shirt fell to the floor along with his jeans. His phone and wallet were left on the nightstand next to the right side of the bed he had subtly claimed as his.

We got into bed, and once we were under the sheets, I snuggled into his side, my head preferring his shoulder as a pillow, my arm gripping him like he was a teddy bear and not an enormous, hard man. My leg tucked between his, and I closed my eyes, my anxious heart finally slowing down now that the worst was over.

A quiet breath escaped his lips as his fingers gently slid into my hair, his lips near my forehead. His arm moved over mine, his fingers interlocking with mine on his stomach. There was never a time when he walked through the door and didn't want me. That was usually his only reason for coming at all. But now, sex seemed to be the last thing on his mind, either because he was too tired or just didn't care about it at the moment.

That was fine with me. I just wanted him right now, to know he was alive at my fingertips.

I expected him to question me about what I did, to grin and make a smartass comment, to remind me that I broke my own promise just a few weeks after I made it.

But he didn't.

I WOKE up to the sound of him getting out of bed.

The bed shifted then sprang back up once his weight had left the mattress. He was quiet as he left the bedroom, but his heavy footsteps became audible once he stepped onto the hardwood floor.

My hand reached for him even though I knew he was gone, and when I felt nothing but the warm sheets he'd left behind, I opened my eyes, my vision blurry, and saw that he was really gone. He told me he would never leave without saying goodbye, so the panic dispersed and I turned back to the clock on my nightstand to see the time.

It was noon.

I wanted to go back to sleep, but now that I knew he was gone, I was too uncomfortable. I went into the bathroom and washed my face and brushed my teeth before I fixed my hair and joined him in the kitchen.

He opened my cabinets and searched through my groceries until he found pancake mix. Then he opened the fridge and grabbed the almost empty carton of eggs along with the carton of milk.

I stared at his muscled back and the way his boxers hung low on his hips. His enormous arms effortlessly lifted the carton of milk that sometimes required both of my hands to lift when it was completely full. "Morning."

He finished turning on the burners on the stove before he looked at me over his shoulder. "Hey, baby."

I wrapped my arms around his waist and kissed his shoulder, the thick muscle that was dark with ink.

His hand reached back to grip my ass, and he kissed my hairline. "You need to go shopping. If you're gonna have a man like me, you're gonna have to feed him."

"You sound like a bear."

"Because I am."

When I turned away, I noticed a pile of cash on the counter. "What's this?"

"For groceries."

I raised an eyebrow then turned back to him. "I can afford my own groceries."

He poured the batter into the pan, the food sizzling as it cooked, and then turned back to me. "I'm the one eating everything."

"So? You're my guest."

He turned to me, his good mood fading as he grew annoyed. "Take the money. That's final."

"That's final?" I crossed my arms and raised an eyebrow, appalled by the way he laid down the law like a dictator—in my own fucking home.

He quickly flipped the pancake before he came toward me, making me step back automatically as he cornered me between the two sets of cabinets. When there was nowhere else for me to go, he raised his arms and gripped both edges of the countertop so I really couldn't escape. "I'm your man. I take care of you. Not the other way around."

"I thought a partnership was equal."

"Not with me." He turned back to the stove and finished cooking. "How many pancakes do you want?"

I let the argument die because he really did eat a lot, and I simply didn't have the disposable income to feed him all the time. But I was so stubborn that I wouldn't admit that. "One is fine."

"Grab some plates. And get these eggs ready."

I rolled my eyes as he bossed me around, but I did as he asked. We fell into quiet harmony as we worked together, making breakfast at lunchtime. We had scrambled eggs and pancakes and left all the dirty pans on the stove as we sat together at my cheap table.

He poured syrup over his high stack of pancakes and sprinkled pepper into his eggs. With elbows on the table, he ate like he was starving, shoveling food into his mouth with his eyes on his plate.

I only had a drop of syrup and still didn't eat much of my meal. I had half of the pancake and picked at the eggs. I noticed I'd gained some weight since I'd started seeing Heath exclusively, from all the meals we had when I wouldn't have eaten anything at all. It wasn't enough to alarm me or affect my performance, but if I continued to let it happen, my outfits for the ballet would no longer fit and I would have a problem. "When are you going to invite me to your place?"

It was a four-seater cheap table, so he sat in the chair next to me, slightly turned my way. He grabbed his coffee and took a drink. "I already said you can come whenever you want. I gave you a key." He leaned back in the chair and looked into the living room, spotting the golden key that he'd left on the table a week ago.

"I'm not you. I'm not just gonna barge in."

"Well, you should."

I'd been to his house once, but I only saw a small part of it. I had no idea what went on in that place, what I might walk in on. "What if I walk in there and—"

He stopped eating and gave me a fierce look. "I have nothing to hide." His deep voice shattered the comfort of our conversation, reminding me that he was a wild bull who could rear its head at any moment. "Come and go as you please. I mean that."

I did like this transparency, that he didn't play games like other men. According to my friends, most men treated commitment like a disgusting disease, but Heath opened himself to me completely. "I just meant with your line of work...is that a safe place for me to be?"

His wrath diminished. "Probably the safest place in the world. I have a lot of different residences that I visit across the city, so if anyone is watching me, it's hard to figure out where I actually live. And my homes have the highest level of protection. I'll give you the address." He continued to eat, placing large bites in his mouth.

"I remember where you live."

"You saw it one time." His eyes were on his food. "And you weren't in the right state of mind."

"I have a photographic memory."

He stopped chewing for a moment, his eyes immediately flicking back to me. He finished his bite and swallowed. "Really?"

I nodded. "I can look at something once and recall it in detail for a long period of time. So, yes, I remember where you live."

"Why didn't you mention this before?"

I pushed aside my half-eaten plate and brought my coffee closer. "I don't know... We don't talk much."

He stared at me for a while as if he was impressed, then continued to eat. "Does Damien have a photographic memory?"

"No."

"Makes sense. You seem to be a lot more intelligent than he is."

It was a comment I would make to my brother myself, but my eyes narrowed at the insult.

"You are. I don't feel bad for saying it." He finished everything on his plate when he scooped his last big bite into his mouth. "And it's pretty hot...being with a smart woman."

And just like that, I stopped being mad at him.

He pulled his phone out of his pocket and typed something on a blank page before he pushed it toward me. It was a combination of eight numbers.

I looked at it. "What is that?"

"The code to the main doors." He pulled the phone back. "Enter that into the keypad first."

"Then what's the key for?"

"The second security check. The code unlocks a different set of locks, but you need the key to open the final one. That way, no one can just hack in to my system." He slipped the phone back into his pocket and continued to drink his coffee.

Now that Damien had been mentioned, I knew it was only a matter of time before Heath mentioned the events that transpired last night. But he leaned back in the chair, showing sleepy eyes and a relaxed position, like that was the last thing on his mind. His fingers were wrapped around the handle of his mug as he stared at my stove.

Maybe he wasn't going to mention it.

My eyes roamed over his body, the body I'd touched last night. He didn't seem to have a single scar from whatever had happened, getting out of the situation completely untouched. I just hoped Damien had met the same fate. "I think I'm gonna see him today...check on him."

His eyes moved back to mine. "I had to hit him a couple times, but he's fine. Minor injuries."

"I know, but..."

"And how will you explain your visit?"

I shrugged. "I stop by to see my father all the time. It's not unusual."

When I mentioned my father, he looked away.

"And you're okay?"

He stared at his coffee for a few seconds before he turned back to me, his blue eyes noticeably brighter in the morning as the sunlight came through the windows. "I'm fine, baby." He held my gaze for a second before he turned back to his coffee and took a drink.

I hated how much I cared about him, how he softened me so quickly. It'd only been a few weeks, and I cared for him as much as I cared about my own family. How did this happen?

"I have to go." He rose from his seat and carried the dishes to the sink.

I was disappointed, but I was also anxious to see Damien, to see that he was well with my own eyes.

He cleared my plate too but left my coffee behind before he walked into the bedroom and put on his clothes.

I hated watching him leave. It was painful every time for whatever reason.

When he returned, I got out of my chair and met him by the front door, wearing little shorts and my usual tank. I could tell his mood was different after what had happened last night, but I couldn't determine how, couldn't figure out how he felt about everything. I didn't ask because I didn't want him to ask me in return.

His hand slid into my hair, and he tilted my chin up so our gazes could lock. His large hand overtook my neck and my jawline, warm and demanding, and it was so sexy when he touched me this way, wasn't afraid to claim me as his. "Come over tonight."

The pain of his departure was suddenly gone, and now I wasn't afraid of how he felt about last night. He didn't push me away. He didn't put up any walls. He wasn't afraid of what my gesture meant. "Alright."

"I should be home around seven. Come by any time after that."

"Alright."

He leaned down and gave me a purposeful kiss with those demanding lips, moving my mouth with his, gently pulling my bottom lip between his before he breathed into me. His hand pulled away first, and he opened his eyes to stare at me, as if he loved the look in my eyes when I kissed him.

Then he pulled away.

I let him go, paralyzed by how good that kiss was.

After he opened the door, he gave me a playful smack on the ass then headed down the hallway.

I watched him walk away like I always did, missing him more and more the farther away he was.

TWO

CATALINA

I joined my father for a late lunch even though I'd just eaten, sitting across from him in the dining room as the sun blanketed the floor from the windows. The warm weather of summer was still here, but it was fading fast, the days not nearly as long as they used to be. "Damien won't be joining us?"

He shrugged as he continued to eat his salad. "Patricia said he's busy today."

"So, he went to work?"

"I don't think so. He usually has coffee with me before he goes."

That wasn't a good sign. "I'll stop by and say hello before I go."

He poured more blue cheese dressing on his salad even though he clearly had enough.

"Dad." I grabbed the dressing bottle and pulled it away. "What's the point in eating a salad if you're gonna drown it in dressing?"

"What's the point in eating a salad at all?" he barked. "Lettuce doesn't taste like anything." He didn't reach for the dressing again, but he wasn't happy about it. "Patricia is a great cook, but all this healthy shit is overrated. Every time I ask her to make me a burger, she gives me this vegan bullshit —with no cheese. What is that? She always says she's out of real beef burgers, but I don't buy that. Damien is running this place like a goddamn prison."

I had a lot more respect for my brother for taking my father in. He was a sweet man, but when it came to food, he could lose his temper easily. When he lived alone, all he ate were frozen dinners and fast food. His blood pressure was through the roof, and his waistline was growing. He'd put on some weight when he first moved in with Damien. But now that he'd been here for a few months, he'd lost at least twenty pounds. "I think your son has been really generous taking you in. You have everything you need, someone to make your bed every morning and clean up after you, and your son is in the same house if you need anything."

He seemed to be embarrassed after he heard what I said. He dropped his gaze and sighed. "You're right, I'm sorry. I just miss eating the way I used to…"

"Well, you can't. That's just how it is."

He grabbed his fork and flicked off all the extra dressing he'd added, finally complying.

I smiled. "That's better."

AFTER LUNCH, I went to the third floor and knocked on Damien's bedroom door.

"What?" His deep voice was full of irritation.

Geez, he was in a bad mood. He had no idea if it was Patricia or his father, and he still spoke that way.

I opened the door and poked my head inside. He sat at the dining table shirtless, his laptop in front of him, a scowl on his face. "Just wanted to stop by and say hello."

His eyes pulled away from his screen, and he glanced at me, his fingertips resting against his lips. His expression didn't change as he looked at me.

My eyes immediately surveyed his appearance, making sure he wasn't seriously injured.

He rose from the chair and walked into his closet.

I stared at his bare back, not seeing anything alarming.

When he returned, he was wearing a shirt, covering up his nakedness in front of me. That scowl was still part of his expression, like the last thing he wanted to do was visit with me. He sank back into the chair. "How's Dad?"

I walked over to the chair across from him, and now that I was closer, I could tell that he'd been struck in the head. There was a dark discoloration under his hair, like he had a fresh scar. I tried not to stare at it too much, to wear my heart on my sleeve. "Hates the food..."

"What's new?"

"He tried to pour the entire bottle of dressing on his salad. I told him to knock it off."

"Yes. He's been asking for a burger every week since he moved in here."

"Yeah, he mentioned that."

His gaze turned back to his laptop.

So, I stared at his injury further, telling myself that it was nothing for a strong man like him.

"Yes?" His eyes darted back to me.

"What?" I asked, caught off guard.

"You keep staring at me."

"Well...you look like someone hit you in the head with a crowbar. Are you okay?"

He sighed and closed his laptop. "I'm fine."

"Then why aren't you at work?"

"Because I don't have to go to work," he snapped. "I can do whatever the fuck I want."

He was really pissed about last night. I'd sabotaged his plan, and now he was furious it didn't work out the way he wanted. It was all my fault...and I felt so fucking guilty. The bruise on his head was because of me. "I just...want to make sure you're okay. I love you." The words tumbled out of my mouth before I could stop them.

His eyes were less hostile. "Cat, I'm gonna be fine. I'm not dying."

"I know… I just hate seeing you hurt."

"I'm not hurt. It'll heal."

"What happened?"

He stared at me for a long time before he answered. "Just work bullshit. But it's fine. It's just a setback."

"A setback?"

"Yeah. I'll take care of it later."

So, Damien wasn't going to stop. He was going to keep fighting Heath forever. "Maybe you should just let this go—"

"Maybe you should mind your own business." His voice rose, echoing in the large room as he gave me a cold stare.

"I just care about you, alright?" I countered. "I don't want you to get yourself killed. Why don't you just retire? You're gonna ask Anna to marry you. Hades retired, so why don't you?"

"Hades and I aren't the same person."

"Then maybe you should be the same person. Come on. Think about it."

He shook his head. "You've never been worried about me before, so where is this coming from?"

I tried to think of something fast. "Anna was captured. Some guy broke in to your home. You had to fight some guy in a death match. Yeah, I'm fucking worried. You have plenty of money, and if you really don't want to be home, keep working at the bank. But there's more to life than your business. You and Anna could travel. You could start a family. There're so many things you can do."

"Quit ballet."

I turned quiet, my eyebrow raised. "What?"

"What if I told you to quit ballet? You could break an ankle...a knee."

"Not the same thing—"

"It is the same thing," he snapped. "I built this empire, and I'm not gonna walk away from it yet. I told Anna I would leave once we start our family, but not before. She accepted that, the woman I'm gonna marry, so I don't see why it matters to you."

"It matters to me because I fucking love you, Damien." My voice rose. "I want you to live a very long time. I want you to be an uncle to my kids. I want to be an aunt to yours. It matters to me a lot."

His anger was sheathed. "Don't worry about me. I'm fine."

"You don't look fine."

"Trust me, this is nothing. I've been through much worse."

"Is that supposed to make me feel better?" I snapped. "You're just proving my point, Damien."

He sighed in irritation, his gaze moving out the window. "I appreciate your concern, but let it go."

"You're the one who needs to let this vendetta go, Damien."

He turned his gaze back to me, his eyes cold. "Would you let it go? If there was a man you loved and someone took him away from you, would you fucking let it go?"

I inhaled a deep breath because one man popped into my head, but I had to force him away, not allowing this man to have a face... and definitely not to have blue eyes and an intense stare. "You have Anna and you're happy. That's all that matters. Leave the past in the past."

He shook his head in disappointment. "I never let anything go. And I'm not gonna let this fucking go either."

———

I HAD practice at the theatre, so I didn't get to Heath's place until nine. I parked at the curb and walked up the steps until I arrived at his front door. There were two doors, both deep brown and ordinary. It didn't seem like they were thick enough to stop a militia from getting inside, but I knew it was probably all for show, so when kids came to the door selling candy they wouldn't have a clue what they'd walked into.

There was a camera in each corner, protected by a thick frame of glass, probably encased in bulletproof material. A keypad was on the wall, black and sleek. I typed in the long combination then heard the sound of air compressors erupting from behind the door, the same sound a safe made once it unlocked.

Then I slipped the ordinary key inside and got the doors unlocked.

When I opened the door, I came into contact with a metal wall. The wooden door had opened outward onto the street, but the metal one swung inward. When I started to push it, I realized how heavy it was, and then I realized it was several feet thick.

Whoa.

I stepped inside the house and shut both sets of doors. When the metal door was shut, the mechanisms inside immediately came to life, clicking and locking as all the bolts within it returned to place.

Shit, he wasn't fucking around.

I turned around and saw a sitting area in front of a fireplace. It looked untouched, like it was staged for visual purposes. To the right were the stairs that led down to the basement.

The basement where he'd kept me.

I couldn't believe I was there again...under completely different circumstances.

There was another set of steps in front of me, so I walked up until I emerged into a large living room, floor-to-ceiling windows comprising one entire wall. Everything was modern and sleek, like it had been renovated recently.

He didn't seem to be anywhere.

I explored his place, seeing the three couches that faced a large TV on the wall. Shelves were on either side of it, and he had unusual sculptures, all made of gray metal. A large fireplace was against one wall.

I kept moving, coming across an enormous kitchen, a fridge with a glass door, and an island bigger than my

entire kitchen. My hand dragged across the granite coun-
tertops before I stepped into the hallway. There was
another set of stairs that led to another floor, but I looked
down the opposite hallway, assuming that was where his
bedroom was located. I wanted to put my bag down, but it
seemed presumptuous to enter his private bedroom
without permission, even though he claimed not to care.
"Heath?"

No response.

I set my bag on one of the couches and took the stairs to the
next level. There was another sitting area, but smaller than
the first. I moved down the hallway and saw glass walls that
enclosed a private gym.

It was decked out with all kinds of equipment, from cardio
machines to full weight machines.

Then I spotted him lying flat, picking up a bar stacked with
weights as he did his bench presses, letting the heavy weight
sink to his chest before he pushed it back into the air, strug-
gling but completing the set.

Shirtless and covered in sweat, he had clearly been working
out for a while. Black headphones covered his ears. He
racked the bar and lay there for a bit, catching his breath
before he grabbed the bar again, his hands protected by
thick black gloves, and he did another set, breathing in a
timely matter as he raised and lowered the weights. He was
in black running shorts and workout shoes, his sculpted
thighs and calves visible.

I watched him for a while, my heart beating quick and my
palms beginning to sweat. His arms were so strong, thick
from his shoulders all the way down to his forearms. When

his skin was shiny with sweat, he looked even sexier, like this was some kind of free porn.

Jesus, he was hot.

I walked through the door and slowly came toward him, not wanting to alarm him because he obviously had no idea I was there. I moved behind him and let him finish. I didn't mind waiting with a view like this. I wore a red dress with heels, my hair done because I'd planned to come over here after work.

When he was finished with his set, he sat up and wiped his face with his towel. With his arms on his knees, he leaned forward, his eyes on the ground. After a few seconds, he raised his gaze to look at himself in the mirror.

His eyes moved to mine immediately.

His face was tinted red from exertion, new beads of sweat forming the second he wiped his face. His chest rose and fell deeply because he was still tired. He didn't give a flash of alarm at my unexpected presence, always calm. His eyes looked me over, trailing down my body to my heels, appreciating the way I looked. Then he pulled the headphones off his head. "Damn." When he wore his intense expressions, he was difficult to read, so it was sexy when he spoke his mind. He set the headphones aside and rose to his feet, his muscles pumped with blood after his workout.

I walked to him, my heels loud against the hardwood floor. I couldn't believe this six-foot-three hunk was mine, that I got to enjoy the most masculine man on this planet.

He didn't lean down and kiss me or touch me. "I'll give you a better greeting after I rinse off."

"I don't mind." My palms flattened against his sweaty chest, my fingertips immediately soaked from the moisture. I moved into him and kissed his sweaty lips, tasting the potent salt on my tongue.

He kissed me back but still didn't touch me, like he didn't want my dress or hair dirty. But he could still kiss me well without cupping my neck or my cheek, could rely on his lips to make my knees tremble.

My hands slowly streaked down his chest, making pathways in his sweat. I could feel his muscles twitch from his work-out, feel how much heat his body naturally produced. I pulled his bottom lip into my mouth and gave him a gentle bite before I pulled away.

Now, his gaze had darkened, as if I had the exact effect on him as he did on me, as if I could floor him with a simple embrace. He leaned down and pressed a kiss to my neck, wiping his sweat on my skin before he pulled away. He grabbed his headphones, water, and towel from the floor and walked out with me. "I'll take a shower, and we'll have dinner."

"I'd prefer it if you fucked me first."

He turned to me, his lips slightly raised in a smile at my bluntness. "Whatever my woman wants."

We took the stairs back down to the second floor, and on the way, I grabbed my bag that I'd left on the couch. He walked beside me as he guided me down the hallway to his bedroom. The door was already open, so he stepped inside, revealing a sleek master bedroom. One side of the room was all floor-to-ceiling windows, and discreetly tucked at the top were the shades that would roll down and cover everything so he could block out the sunlight and sleep in. A king-size bed was against the wall, covered in a gray comforter that matched his gray-stained hardwood floors. He had a large TV on the wall, a desk in the corner that had his laptop, and a big walk-in closet. On the other side of the room was an entryway that led to a large bathroom.

I walked to his dresser and set my bag on top.

He took his clothes into the closet, tossing them in the dirty laundry bin for someone to wash later. His closet wasn't stuffed with suits and ties like my brother's was. It was full of plain t-shirts and jeans, a few long sleeves and sweaters, along with a couple jackets. He was a simple man with simple tastes. "Make yourself comfortable." He headed into the bathroom.

I watched him walk away, buck naked, and that tight ass was incredible. No way was I going to stay in the bedroom alone when there was a fine piece of man about to get into the shower. I followed him.

He had a large shower with glass doors, and he was already inside under the warm water, rubbing a bar of soap every-where, cleaning every inch of his skin, lathering his dick and cleaning his balls. Even when he was soft, he still had a nice dick, distinct and long.

I sat on the toilet and watched the show.

He shampooed his hair, rinsed, and then turned off the water, just as sexy wet as he was when he was sweaty. He pushed the door open and grabbed the towel, noticing me sitting there. He gave a slight smile then dried off before he stepped onto the mat in front of the shower. "You're eager."

I shrugged. "I know what I want."

"Damn right." He scrubbed the towel over his hair last before he hung it back on the rack, to be reused tomorrow.

I got to my feet and walked out of the bathroom, knowing he was right behind me. I sat on the bed and scooted back before I lay flat, placing my heels against his bare chest. His bed was higher than mine, the perfect level for him to stand and fuck me deep.

He grabbed one ankle then loosened the strap on my shoe so he could slip it off. He did the same with the other before he pushed up my dress around my hips and grabbed my panties. I lifted my hips as he pulled the panties down over my thighs and to my feet. When they were off, he left them on the bed, like he wanted to see them in his periphery while he fucked me. "This is how you want it?" He grabbed my hips and dragged me down so my ass hung over the edge. He pulled my knees apart so I was open to him, our bodies close together.

My hands flattened against his abs, and I bit my bottom lip as I nodded. "I want to look at you…"

He stared down at me with his beautiful eyes, so bright but so dark at the same time. He was a pretty man, but he was so hard in every other way that he looked vicious. Without wetting himself, he guided his dick to my entrance and moistened his tip that way, smearing himself in the moisture that had already soaked my panties from watching him in the shower. Then he slid inside, inching farther and farther until only a few inches remained outside my body.

I closed my eyes and moaned, like it was the first time all over again. I grabbed his hips and pulled him a little farther, wincing when his size started to hurt me. I opened my eyes again, watching him grow even more turned on as he watched me hurt myself on purpose, wanting all of him regardless of the pain.

He started to rock into me, sliding his dick inside me over and over, his balls lightly tapping against my ass at the end of every thrust. His hands continued to grip my hips and hold me still as he moved inside me, giving me that fat dick like I was the only woman he wanted to give it to.

His expression tightened, as if watching me enjoy him was an additional turn-on. He started to move faster and harder, tugging me as he thrust at the same time.

I held on to his hips and pushed myself forward, slamming into him with the same desire, my legs opened and my tits shaking from our movements. "Heath..." My head rolled back, and I was suddenly pulled under by the goodness, by the explosion between my legs.

He watched me until I finished, controlling himself so I could enjoy every second before he brought it to an end.

"Wait..." My nails dug into his skin. "Not yet..."

He stopped for a moment, his eyes locked and focused. But he obeyed and started to move again. "Yes, baby."

THREE

HEATH

I FLIPPED THE CHICKEN IN THE PAN AS I STOOD AT THE stove. Catalina looked out the floor-to-ceiling window to the city at her feet. She was in one of my shirts, so big that it fit her like a blanket. I glanced at her as I listened to the food sizzle in the hot oil, staring at her long, curled hair as it trailed down her back. She looked good in my shirt, and she looked even better in my house.

Like she belonged there.

When the meat started to sizzle louder, I turned back to what I was doing and flipped it again. The asparagus cooked in a different pan, so I flipped that too. "It's almost ready."

She flinched slightly at my words, as if she'd forgotten I was there, forgotten what she was doing. She slowly turned around and looked at me, her expression tight, like there was a demon locked inside her chest, haunting her.

I turned off the burners and set down the spatula, knowing whatever she was about to say next was important.

She came close to me, her eyes defeated, her posture poor like she'd been beaten in combat. She dropped her gaze, thinking about her words before she said them. "I need you to do something for me..."

Without knowing what the request was, I already knew my answer. "Anything."

She dropped her gaze again, opening and closing her lips like she wanted to speak but just couldn't get the words out. "Promise me you'll never hurt my brother...no matter what happens with us."

I hadn't asked her if she'd visited her family today because I preferred not to think about them, to see Catalina as her own woman with no attachment to my enemies. But she must have seen Damien today, saw the bruise on his head, witnessed his rage after his plan unraveled with a simple phone call. She probably felt guilty that she was the reason her brother had lost the battle, knowing he would have won if she'd kept her mouth shut.

She searched my gaze as she waited for an answer.

"He's not going to let it go, is he?" I gave Damien so many chances, but he was emotional and stupid, holding a grudge like a knife in his grasp. I did everything I could to spare his life, found other ways to punish him when I never would have considered them in the first place.

She shook her head.

I turned away, frustrated that this motherfucker was making my life difficult, making me shoot one of my own men to protect his pathetic life.

"Please," she whispered. "I saved your life…"

I stared at the stove as I took a deep breath, frustrated by her words. "Baby, I would make you that promise even if you hadn't done what you did." I straightened and turned back to her.

She moved into me, cupping my face as she pressed her forehead to my chin. "Thank you."

I abandoned the food altogether and wrapped my arms around her waist, pulling her close so I could hold her in the kitchen, feel her soul, smell her scent. Every moment of the day, I felt like a strong man, but whenever she was in my arms, I felt inexplicably weak. She was my undoing, the rose petals to my thorns.

She clung to me in relief, like my promise meant the world to her because she knew I would keep it. Maybe she thought it balanced the scales for her brother, since she'd betrayed him. Her arms circled my neck, and she held me in my kitchen, the sexiest woman to stand there, the only woman to ask me for something and actually get it.

When I'd answered the call and she confessed the truth, I didn't have much time to dwell on her decision. I had to act fast. Otherwise, I would die anyway. But when everything was said and done, I still didn't think about it, and I didn't ask her either. Her feelings were pretty clear. Why talk about them?

She pulled away slowly, her arms sliding down until her hands cupped the back of my neck. But then she took those away too, looking at me with the softest green eyes. She hardly showed her fire anymore because she was completely tame. I was no danger to her, no threat whatso-ever, so she changed...let me see her in a new way.

She seemed embarrassed by what she'd just asked me to do. Timid, she stood there and tucked her beautiful hair behind her ear. Her lips were plump and full, the single freckle on her face so damn sexy. "Can I help?" She turned to the stove.

If she wanted to pretend that moment hadn't just happened, fine. But it did happen—and we both knew it. I turned the burners back on. "Grab a couple of plates." I heated the chicken and stirred the vegetables, and once everything was done, I scooped the meal onto the dishes.

She carried the plates to the table right next to the window, a table that could easily hold ten people. Then she looked through my cabinets, probably searching for a bottle of wine. "Wow, you've got a lot of vodka..."

"I'll take a glass."

She grabbed a bottle and searched my fridge for a mixer. When she found a bottle of cranberry juice in the fridge, she mixed it. Then she picked a bottle of wine and poured it for herself. "Why do you like vodka so much?"

"Because I've drunk a lot of it." I sat at the table and watched her place the glass in front of me before she took the seat across from me, the view of the city in her line of sight. "I used to live in Russia."

She was about to cut into her chicken, but she flinched at what I said. "What?"

"Yeah." I kept eating, not stopping for the conversation because I was starving. I usually ate right after my workout, but she got on my bed and told me to fuck her, and no amount of hunger was going to get me to walk away from that.

"When?"

"A few years ago. I lived there for about two years."

"Why?"

"What's next?" I asked with a chuckle. "How and where?"

When she realized all her questions, she smiled. "Sorry, I'm just surprised."

"I worked there with a crew. Drugs."

"Oh..." She didn't know what to say to that, so she continued to cut into her meat and vegetables. "How did you end up here?"

"My brother. But I got into some bad shit while I was there, and it was a problem for him since he was the Skull King at the time, so he threw me in jail for six months."

"Really?" she asked, her eyebrow raised. "You?"

I nodded.

"What was that like? If you don't mind me asking..."

"Boring."

"Boring?" she asked, surprised by my description.

"Yeah. Same routine every day. I worked out like crazy."

She still seemed shocked by the news. "I can't believe I'm sleeping with a former inmate."

"If you think that's my worst attribute..." I released a quiet chuckle before I continued to eat.

"So, he let you out?"

"Yes, when I cleaned up my act. I moved in with him and became one of the Skull Kings."

"And you just worked until you got promoted?"

"Basically."

"What was the first thing you did when you got out of jail?"

The truth was crass, but I refused to lie to her. I knew exactly who I was, and I wasn't afraid to show my true colors. "Drank beer and fucked a whore." I kept eating like I'd said nothing odd, watching her expression.

She didn't have one. She stabbed her meat with her fork and placed it in her mouth, chewing slowly. "Your place is really nice..." She sidestepped the comment, like she didn't want to picture me fucking some woman I paid.

"Thank you."

"It's very...you."

When I finished all the food on my plate, I enjoyed my vodka. "I'm glad you like it. Hope you come over often."

"Depends."

"On?"

"How comfy that bed is."

"You've already lain on it."

"Yeah, but I wasn't paying much attention."

"Well, if you don't like it, you can just sleep on me."

She smiled before she pulled her wine closer to her. "I guess that's true."

AT THE END of the night, we went into my bedroom. It was a spacious room, much bigger than her bedroom in that small apartment. I was definitely more comfortable over here, but as long as I got to be with her, it didn't matter where we were.

She moved to the corner of the room, stilled, and then sprinted to my bed. She jumped high and landed on the mattress, bouncing slightly.

I watched her with a serious expression, finding her child-like behavior comical even if I didn't show it.

"Oh my god, this bed is huge." She rolled over and stretched her arms and legs out, like she was making a snow angel in my sheets.

"Well, I'm a big guy." I dropped my sweatpants and set my phone on the nightstand. There was a pistol in my night-stand and a shotgun under my bed. I turned off the lights then hit the buttons to the shutters, closing all the windows so the sunlight wouldn't bother us in the morning.

She sat up and watched them closely. "Wow...that's so cool." Like a child, she was impressed by everything.

I got into bed and lay there, watching her continue to examine things in my bedroom.

She eventually got out of bed then walked to my closet. "Can I look around?"

I gave her the same answer I always gave. "I have nothing to hide."

"Okay, but I'm not snooping. Just looking." She flicked on the light and stepped inside. She looked at all my shirts and jeans then opened one of the drawers. The light immediately came on and revealed an assortment of guns and ammunition. She stilled in surprise before she gently shut the drawer. When she opened the next one, she found the same thing, but there were also grenades and blades. "Whoa." She shut the drawer then stepped out again. "Never piss you off."

"The world shouldn't piss me off. But you can." I liked it, being with a woman who wasn't afraid to speak her mind unapologetically.

She grabbed her bag from the dresser. "I'm gonna get ready for bed." She walked into the bathroom.

She didn't have any special bedtime routines, so I thought that announcement was odd, but I didn't question it. Maybe she had something personal to take care of, to take her birth control pills or something.

I lay there and closed my eyes, the sheets around my waist because I was always hot, regardless of how low the setting was for my AC. I'd had women over here before, but I usually fucked whores at their place in case they tried to steal from me. But it was rare, to meet a woman I liked enough to bring to my private headquarters.

Minutes later, she stepped out of the bathroom, and instead of having a clean face with no makeup like she was ready to sleep, she was in a sexy piece of lingerie. A black bodysuit made of lace that barely hid her tits from view. With her long hair in curls down her sides and her makeup heavier than it'd been earlier, she looked like she was ready to take my dick good even though she'd already had it hours ago.

I propped myself up on my elbows so I could see her better, let my eyes trail over her body to the open crotch that made her cunt accessible without undressing. A woman had never put on lingerie for me before.

This was a first.

And damn.

She studied my reaction to her, and she seemed to like what she saw, because she suddenly became more confident, her knees hitting the bed before she crawled to me.

I wanted to grab her and fuck her so damn hard, but I was paralyzed, letting her decide how this played out. My cock was instantly hard under my sheets and started to poke through.

She kept moving until she was on top of me, her long hair trailing along my chest as she crept closer. When her face was above mine, she went for my bottom lip, pulling it into her mouth and giving it a gentle bite that made me nearly bleed. Then she kissed my neck, moved over my chest, and made her way down my hard abs until she grabbed the sheet in her teeth and pulled it off my dick.

My hands tightened into fists, and I stayed still even though I knew where this was going, knew that sweet mouth would be around my dick at any moment, sucking and licking like it was candy. I've had my dick sucked so many times, but the excitement never wore off, and since it was Catalina, my excitement was explosive.

With her ass in the air, she leaned down and started to kiss my balls, gently dragging her tongue over my sensitive skin before she sucked it into her mouth, kissing, licking, her eyes locked on mine like my dick was her lover and I was prying.

My breathing slowly increased the longer she kissed me, my firm chest rising and falling a little deeper because my lungs needed more air. My hands formed fists because I was tense, my dick so hard it started to ache. I thought lying back and enjoying the sexiest woman in the world eat my dick would be easy, but I had to fight all my instincts to grab her and flip her over. I liked to be in charge, but I forced myself to surrender.

She dragged her tongue up my length, right over the thick vein, and moved until she reached the tip. Then she kissed the head, swiping her tongue over the precome that started to seep out. Her eyes opened and closed, like she was really making out with my dick, replacing my lips with another part of my body.

When I took another breath, the moan I released was unstoppable. I was a quiet lover because I preferred to listen to the woman tell me what she liked, but I found myself enjoying sex more than usual because my partner was equally giving, equally talented.

She kissed my dick as she stared into my eyes, her eyes filled with more arousal than mine, like she wanted nothing more than to make love to my dick with her tongue. If ballet didn't work out and she wanted to be a whore, she could charge anything she wanted—and get every coin she asked for.

She opened her mouth and flattened her tongue before she slid down, craning her neck to stick my dick in her throat. She moved as far as she could, leaving a few inches out because it simply wasn't possible to take it all. She kept her ass in the air, her back arched like a tiger, and moved up and down my length, her spit dripping to my balls.

Fuck, I already wanted to come.

She took it slow, like she wanted me to last a long time, to enjoy every minute before I couldn't take it any longer.

But my threshold had disappeared once we skipped the condoms, once our commitment had deepened into a relationship I'd never had before. Now there was only one woman in my life, and even when I was out with the boys while she was asleep, I didn't even look. I turned down offers all the time. My usual girls texted me because I was their favorite client, but I wasn't remotely enticed.

This was all I wanted.

She lifted her gaze and watched me as she struggled to keep going without making herself choke. She had to crane her neck to move up and down without changing her position, encouraging me to enjoy the view of her perky cheeks in the air.

I wanted to keep going. I wanted to lie there and just enjoy it. But watching this woman do everything for me, be a fantasy I didn't even ask for, made me want more of her... made me want to be inside her, to rock my headboard into the wall while I looked her in the eye, enjoying the woman who gave herself to me completely.

The woman who wasn't afraid.

My hand went to her neck, and I lifted her, making her drop my dick so it landed with a wet thud against my abs. I pulled her to me, bringing her mouth to mine for a slow kiss. My hands finally got to touch her, to feel the texture of the lace. My hands followed her curves, followed her hips to her narrow waist. My thumbs stretched across her chest, resting underneath the swells of her tits, feeling her slow heartbeat, like she was absolutely calm when we were together.

I kissed her as her hair fell around me, her perfume overcoming my senses, turning me on more. This intensity was potent, my breath shaky because all my senses were overloaded. My thighs tightened and my dick twitched, my mind living in a reality that seemed too good to be true.

I slowly rolled her over until she was on her back, her head hitting my pillow. "I want to please you..." Her tits were visible through the fabric, and she immediately widened her legs and pulled her knees to her chest, knowing exactly how I would take her.

My arms hooked behind her knees, and I held my face above hers, my dick getting ready to slide through her tight opening and plunge deep inside. "You are." I kissed her again, our lips moving together slowly, taking our time. "This is how I want you." I gradually slid inside her, slowly pushed through her copious wetness, stretched out her tightness. I moaned as I sank deeper and deeper, her spit removing every single hint of friction. I pushed all the way inside her even though it hurt her a bit, made tears emerge in her eyes.

Her hands cupped my face, and she held me close, breathing against my lips as she tolerated my size.

I loved that she let me do this to her, that she wanted all of me, even if it hurt.

I pulled away and started to rock into her normally, to glide in and out gently, stopping before I went too far.

She grabbed my ass and dug her fingers deep, yanking me farther into her, like she wanted it anyway, like she didn't care, like she wanted me to watch the tears streak from the corners of her eyes.

"I don't want to hurt you." I spoke against her mouth, finding this the most erotic moment of my life, to be this connected to another person like this, to share every heartbeat, every thought.

"I want all of you." Her palm planted against my chest, right over my heart. "Exactly as you are..."

WE SPENT the morning and afternoon watching TV on the couch. She was tucked close to my side, her arm around my waist while her cheek rested against my shoulder. We didn't say much, the presence of each other enough. When it was early afternoon, she packed her bag and prepared to leave.

I didn't want her to go.

She was in jeans and a shirt, the outfit she'd packed so she wouldn't have to do the walk of shame in that sexy red dress. She looked up at me, her eyes slightly hinting of dread, like she didn't want to leave either. "I should go..." She echoed my own words back to me, probably understanding the pain I would feel.

Yeah, I felt it. "I'll walk you out." I took the bag off her shoulder and carried it so she wouldn't have to. I took the lead and headed down the stairs to the vault doors. I closed the door behind us and walked her out to the curb to where her car was. When the door was unlocked, I opened the back door and placed her bag inside. "I want you to have this." I pulled out the remote keypad.

She took it, clearly not understanding what it was. She stared at it for a few seconds before she looked at me.

"Enter that same combination so you can get into my garage. I don't want you to park out here." I nodded to the cross street. "The entrance is on the other side."

She nodded. "Alright."

"Come and go as you please." I never gave anyone else access to my home. Not even Steel had it. "I mean that." I had nothing to hide from her. She could walk in any time of the day or night, and I would be happy to see her.

She looked at the sincerity in my gaze before she gave a slight smile. "Okay."

"When are you going to say that to me?" I gave her unlimited access to me, and she still hadn't mirrored that. "Or do you really want me to hand over your key?"

A blush entered her cheeks like she was actually embarrassed by her previous reaction. "No. You already know you're welcome...whether I say it or not."

"Doesn't mean I don't want to hear it."

"Well...come and go as you please." She rose on her tiptoes and grabbed the front of my shirt so she could pull me in for a kiss. She breathed into my mouth hard like the kiss burned her, lit her on fire all over again. Her fingers released my shirt, and she cupped my face, like she wanted more than the street could allow.

My arms wrapped around her and gripped her tight, kissing her hard like I didn't give a damn who saw. One hand gripped her ass, my fingers digging through her jeans to give her a squeeze she wouldn't forget.

When she pulled away, she looked at my lips before she kissed the corner of my mouth. "I'll miss you..."

I cupped the back of her head and rubbed her nose with mine. "Me too, baby."

After a long look, she finally turned away and got into her car.

I watched her drive away.

I SQUATTED DOWN in front of the safe, entering the long combination before I moved to the next step, pressing my palm against the screen to pick up my fingerprints and the webbed lines in the center of my palm. I'd replaced the old-school safe my brother used to use.

The first door opened, and I worked on the next step.

After every security measure was complete, I opened the heavy vault door, a door three times my height.

Steel carried the bags of money inside then used the machines to count everything.

The door behind us was locked, with two armed men protecting the entrance. My men were loyal because they all got a cut of the take, but I was a paranoid man.

Steel started entering the totals into his laptop.

I continued to carry the heavy bags inside before I took the counted bills and organized them in the enormous vault.

"You think Damien will comply next time we see him?"

I kept working, my muscles tight from all the heavy lifting. "Yes." That piece of shit was making my life difficult, and I didn't know what to do. If he pulled a stunt again and I didn't kill him, I would really be in trouble.

"He better. Or you're gonna have to shoot him in the head. Why don't you just do that?"

"He makes us too much money."

Steel shrugged. "It's not that much."

We kept working, spending over an hour taking care of the accounting before we locked the safe door and walked out. We moved down the hallway and entered the main hall, where the men were gathered.

Vox sat there alone, watching me from his place at the table. The look he gave me was different from before, far more sinister, like he was pissed off just to look at my face.

I may have to kill one of my own...and very soon.

FOUR
CATALINA

After our performance, we all went out on the town, hitting up a bar and ordering rounds of drinks. I didn't text Heath because I didn't want to be one of those women who needed her man at her side every moment of the day.

But I definitely wasn't having fun.

Nights like these were the kind I used to live for, to let my hair down and have a good time. But now I saw my friends flirt with guys, get free drinks, and knew their nights would never end up the way mine did.

With a man like Heath.

Sometimes guys hit on me, bought me a drink, but I was quick to tell them I was seeing someone.

And I wasn't interested anyway.

Men I once found attractive were now repulsive. I couldn't believe the guys I'd already slept with; they looked like boys in comparison. Now I sat there alone, my friends involved with their guys, so I was forgotten.

I sipped my cosmo, debating whether I should throw in the towel and go home.

Bars seemed pointless when I wasn't single.

A guy came to my table, a good-looking guy who probably would have scored my phone number if I weren't already seeing someone. He didn't buy me a drink, but he sat beside me and made conversation. "Are you unavailable? I can't imagine any other reason for you to be sitting here alone."

"You guessed right." I drank from my glass, bored out of my mind.

"Well, he's not here, right?" He gave me a playful smile.

Heath and I weren't in a typical romantic relationship, but we were physically committed to each other, and the idea of being with someone else, even if I could get away with it, disgusted me. It felt so wrong, so bad, that it made me physically sick. I raised my hand and gave a flick of my wrist. "I'm not interested."

"Oh, come on." He relaxed in the chair. "I'm just trying to break the ice."

"If you don't leave, I'll break your face." I stared him down so he knew I wasn't joking.

He rolled his eyes and vacated the chair. "Nice talking to you..."

My phone lit up with a message. *Where are you?*

My heartbeat immediately quickened when I saw his name on my screen, heard his deep voice in my head. Instead of being defiant, I gave a straight answer. *At a bar with the girls.*

A lot of guys must be buying you drinks.

Unfortunately.

I'll join you.

Even if he was here, I still didn't want to sit there, surrounded by people who had no idea what we had. *No. I'm gonna leave.*

Because you really hate being seen with me that much?

Reading the text hurt because it was so inaccurate. *No. Because I've been miserable this entire time...because you aren't here.*

I WALKED in the door and spotted him on the couch, already stripped down to his boxers. The TV was on, but his eyes immediately left the screen once I walked inside. He grabbed the remote and hit the button without looking at it before he rose to his feet.

I looked him up and down, having no idea how I'd ever picked up a guy at the bar in the first place. Why would I go out when this man was waiting for me? I tossed my clutch aside as he came closer to me.

He stopped in front of me and looked into my face. "Have a good time?"

I shook my head. "I don't think I can go out with them anymore..."

He stared at me as he waited for an answer.

"There's just nothing for me to do. They hook up with guys they meet, and I just sit there...bored out of my mind. What's the point in going out with them when I would rather be home with you?"

He smiled slightly, one hand moving to my cheek.

My fingers wrapped around his wrist. "I'm not sure if I could ever go back to that...not after you." I didn't know why I said that, why I admitted my deepest thoughts to this man who was only a temporary figure in my life.

His eyes focused harder on my face, hanging on every word I said. "Then don't." His hand moved to the back of my head as he cradled it and leaned down and kissed me. His other arm wrapped around my waist, and he gripped me tightly, touching me in a way no other man had ever done. He squeezed me, suffocated me.

I melted instantly, my arms wrapping around his neck.

His hand lifted my dress until he gripped the back of my thong. He pulled it down over my ass to my thighs and let it fall the rest of the way on its own. Then he picked me up and pinned me against the wall, my legs wrapped around his waist. With his face pressed to mine, he lowered his boxers and shoved himself inside me, sinking deep.

I breathed against his mouth and moaned, my dress hiked to my waist and my ankles locked together with my heels digging into his ass. I loved the way he lifted me effortlessly, the way he slipped inside me without preamble because he didn't need to pause to get a condom on his dick. This man was all mine, and I was all his.

I thought about what that man had said at the bar, that Heath wasn't there to know what I did. I could get away with anything. But I could honestly say there wasn't a single man I wanted more than the man inside me right now.

No one.

HE LAY beside me in bed, naked because the sheets were kicked away. He was over six feet of perfection, his dick still defined even when it was soft. Tattoos marked his fair skin, depicting shadows and demons that accompanied him wherever he went. There was also a skull on his abdomen.

It matched the one on his right hand.

I stared at the huge diamond he wore, watched the way it glittered like it was the most flawless diamond that had ever been mined. "You always wear that?"

His eyes were closed, but they opened when he heard me speak. "Yes."

"Isn't it heavy?"

"I don't notice it."

I reached for his hand and grabbed the ring. "Can I?"

He pulled his hand away and used the fingers of his other hand to twist and pull, getting the tight ring off his finger. It was such a heavy piece of jewelry that he probably needed to always wear it tight. Otherwise, it would fall off. He dropped it in my hand.

It was heavy—really heavy.

I turned it at different angles, examining the unique ring. The diamond was spectacular, the cuts in the surface to represent the eyes. "That's one hell of a ring." I handed it back.

He slipped it back onto his finger, twisted it to get it over his knuckle. "It's definitely a conversation piece."

"Why do you wear it?"

"So people know exactly who I am, even if we've never met."

It surprised me that it never got in the way when we were together, that it didn't get stuck in my hair or scratched my skin when he touched me. He was so used to it that he knew exactly how to carry it.

He reached into the nightstand beside him, grabbing a small black box. "I got something for you."

I stared at the box in his hand, surprised by the gesture. "You don't seem like the kind of man to give a woman jewelry."

He smiled slightly. "I'm not. Open it."

I took it from his hand, assuming it was a ring because the box was too small for a bracelet or necklace. I cracked it open and spotted the stunning diamond inside, displaying the same carvings as his ring.

It was a navel piercing.

I took it out of the box and examined it. "It's beautiful…"

His hand went to my stomach. "I thought it would look sexy…" His thumb brushed over the cheap body jewelry that was there now.

"This is a real diamond…a really nice diamond." I could tell just by looking at it that it was much more expensive than most engagement rings. It was a solid diamond set in white-gold metal, glittering with the same brilliance as his ring.

"Put it on."

I almost couldn't accept it, but it wasn't like he could return it. It was too specific of a gift to return to the jeweler. I removed my old one, which was light and cheap, and then put the new one in.

He stared at it when I was done, his eyes focused on the diamond that perfectly fit inside my small belly button. "Damn." He leaned down and kissed my navel, swiping his tongue over the diamond.

My fingers slid into his hair, and I watched him kiss me, the old jewelry lost somewhere in the bed, forgotten.

His tongue dipped under the piercing, lifting it slightly before he released it. He kissed my stomach as he moved up, gliding through the valley between my tits before his face met mine. He kissed me hard on the mouth as he looked into my gaze. "You like it."

"Yes."

His hand moved to my hip, and he tilted me slightly so he could bring us close together. "Don't ever take it off."

It was probably the most expensive piece of jewelry I'd ever own—and the hottest.

"Alright?" He stared hard into my gaze, as if he'd given me a command that had to be obeyed.

My fingers brushed over his jawline, feeling the stubble that started to grow after he shaved yesterday. "Why would I ever want to take it off?"

A WEEK PASSED, and we developed a routine of sorts.

He would come by whenever he felt like it, letting himself into the apartment without knocking, whether I was there or not. I did the same to him, coming to his place without giving him notice. He was usually watching TV in the living room or working out in his private gym, and not once did he look annoyed by my presence. His blue eyes brightened noticeably whenever I walked through the door.

I was sitting up in bed, reading a book because there was nothing on TV.

The front door opened.

I didn't even flinch because I knew exactly who it was.

"Baby, it's me." He carried bags to the counter then started to open my cabinets and fridge, because he'd picked up groceries on the way. I never asked him to do that. He just did it on his own, even though I was perfectly capable of grabbing my own necessities.

"What did you get?" I asked from my bedroom. We'd fallen into a domestic routine, so comfortable with each other that it became our new way of life.

"Food. And I grabbed your favorite wine—even though it tastes like shit."

I smiled at his deep voice. "Thank you."

He came into the bedroom, looking so sexy in his low jeans and gray shirt. He looked at me and started to strip, removing his thin shirt before getting his jeans loose.

I stopped reading and stared at him.

He grinned slightly, like he enjoyed the attention. "Got something to say?"

"Nope..." I stared at his perfect physique and watched his arms flex as he crawled onto the bed.

He moved on top of me and kissed me, pushing the book away until it thudded on the floor. Then he overtook me completely, making me sink back into the pillows. Anxious, he pushed down his boxers so his dick could be free, and he pulled my panties off, leaving my shirt on because it took too much time to take it off.

Then he slid inside me, both of us slowing down once we were finally connected.

"Yes..." My arms wrapped around his neck, and I released a deep breath, loving how full I felt the second he entered me.

With his forehead to mine, he rocked into me slowly, breathing with me as we enjoyed each other. He moaned quietly from the back of his throat, pausing in his thrusts like he needed a chance to process how good this felt, like he was caught off guard every single time we were together.

"You love this pussy, don't you?" I spoke against his lips, talking dirty even though I never had before.

He moaned in response, louder this time. "This is my pussy..." He started to rock harder, making the headboard tap against the wall. "And I love my pussy."

THE SOUND of falling water was loud because Heath was in the shower just down the hallway. After a few sessions, he was hot and sweaty, and he usually liked to be clean before bed. He continued to shave with my razor instead of bringing his own, even used my toothbrush though he could have grabbed one at the store every time he went.

I picked up my book from the floor and kept reading.

His phone vibrated on the nightstand, lighting up the dark and being obnoxiously loud.

I ignored it.

Then it started to ring.

I kept ignoring it.

Then it vibrated again—and again.

I set my book down because I wondered if something important was happening and Heath needed to know about it. I leaned over his side of the bed and grabbed his phone.

That was when my heart dropped into my chest.

Some bitch named Dynasty texted him a nude picture of herself, her tits in full focus. My hand shook as I stared at it, jealous, angry, pissed, all of the above. It was none of my business, but my emotional response outweighed my pragmatism, and I opened the message box.

Another photo for your collection.

What collection?

I opened his photos next, and he had a whole separate folder for dirty photos...with all kinds of different women. Sometimes the photos were taken with his phone, with the women right beside him.

I felt sick.

I dropped the phone like it burned me.

Now my heart raced, my ears burned from the rise in temperature, and I was so livid I didn't know what to do. I wasn't sure why I was so angry. I didn't think Heath would ever fool around with someone else, but if that wasn't the case, why were women still texting him? Why did he continue to have those photos even though we'd been together for a month now?

What the fuck?

I stormed into the bathroom and yanked on the curtain.

He stilled, looking at me like he had no idea what was going on.

"You fucking asshole." I slapped him across the face then shoved him into the opposite wall.

He was so caught off guard, he nearly fell, gripping the shelf to stabilize himself. "What the fuck?"

I grabbed the bar of soap and threw it at his face. "Piece of shit." I closed the shower curtain and marched off again.

The water turned off, and his footsteps were loud behind me a few seconds later.

I grabbed his clothes off the ground then turned around and threw them in his face. "Get dressed and get the fuck out of my apartment."

He smacked the clothes down when they came at his face, his look full of rage, more furious than he'd ever been. "You care to explain what the hell you're freaking out about—"

I grabbed his phone and pulled up the message. "Who the fuck is Dynasty?"

He didn't look at the screen as it was held up in front of him, his expression hard because he was clearly pissed off at me when I was the only one who should be pissed off.

"'Another photo to add to your collection'?" My voice rose higher and higher since I was so pissed, my chest caved in because I was so hurt. He hurt me—so bad. And that scared me most of all. I panicked, turned dramatic and ridiculous. Just the idea of him looking at another woman made me lose my shit. I pulled up the photo album. "What the fuck are these, Heath?" I threw the phone at his chest, hitting him hard. "How would you feel if I had a bunch of dick pics from all my old lovers? How would you feel if some guy texted me in the middle of the night?"

He let the phone drop to the ground, his chest rising and falling steadily as his face tinted a faint red color. When he spoke, his voice was loud, just like it had been in the basement where he saved me. "Dynasty is one of my whores. I've never hidden my past from you. I've never—"

"If she's part of your past, why is she texting you now? You've been seeing me for over a month, Heath. Why the fuck is this bitch texting you?" My voice matched his, and if we didn't calm down soon, someone was gonna call the cops.

"I can't control what other people do—"

"Why is she texting you?"

His nostrils flared. "No idea. Haven't seen the fucking message."

I rolled my eyes. "Get the fuck out. Don't come back." I kicked his clothes at him.

He didn't move. "You really think I'd mess around?" Now he lowered his voice, turning cold. "You really think I'd do some pussy shit like that?"

"No," I snapped. "And that's why this hurts so much."

"Baby—"

"Don't fucking call me that. I'm not your baby if other women are sending you pictures of their tits."

He stepped closer to me.

I stepped back. "Come near me, and I swear..." I shook my head, ready to strike with everything I had.

He stopped. "I'm one of her best customers, and she's obviously trying to entice me—"

"Would she do that if you told her you were seeing someone?" I snapped. "You obviously haven't told her that."

His nostrils flared again. "I don't explain myself to people. I don't even text her back. I've been so absorbed in you that I forget about the message the second she contacts me."

"Then why do you still have all those pictures on your phone?"

He bowed his head slightly. "I haven't looked at those in a long time. Honestly, I forgot they were even there."

I rolled my eyes again.

"I'm telling you the truth."

"Get the fuck out, Heath." I turned around and walked away, moving to the other side of the bed.

He didn't come after me. He bent down and picked up his phone from the ground. Then he had the audacity to press his thumbs against the screen and text someone.

"May as well tell your whore you'll be there in a few minutes—"

"Shut the fuck up." He lifted his gaze and came toward me, naked with his phone in his hand. He grabbed my wrist and shoved the phone into my hand. "I deleted all the photos. And I texted her back. Look."

Out of defiance, I didn't.

He raised his voice. "Now."

I raised the phone to my face and read the message he'd already sent. *I've got a woman, Dynasty. Don't text me photos anymore, because my woman just saw it and she's losing her fucking mind because she's so head over heels for me that she can't think straight. And I'm just as head over heels for her.*

I couldn't lift my gaze to look at him.

"Scroll up."

"What?"

He pressed his finger to the screen and scrolled up, showing all the times she'd texted him and he never replied.

I dropped the phone and finally looked at him, still pissed.

"Yes, I would be fucking pissed if you had some other guy's junk on your phone. Yes, I'd be pissed if some guy was hitting you up in the middle of the night. But I know you would never mess around on me. Because I trust you." He got closer into my face. "I fucking trust you." His blue eyes pierced into mine. "I admit I should have deleted those photos now that I'm committed to you, but I just forgot about them. You need to trust me, Catalina. Because I'm your man, and as your man, you can trust me—implicitly." He turned away and walked back to his clothes on the floor. He started to get dressed, no longer looking at me. "Let me know when you're ready to apologize."

"Apologize?" I asked incredulously. "You should have told her you were in a relationship. You should have deleted those photos. All of this happened because of you."

He turned back to me, his gaze dark. "You shouldn't have fucking snooped through my phone in the first place."

"Wouldn't have happened if you'd just told the woman you weren't available—"

"And none of this would have happened if you fucking trusted me." He grabbed his wallet and keys off the nightstand. "Yes, I could have handled that better, but so could you. And your response to all of this is far worse than what I did in the first place." He didn't look at me again before he walked out, slamming the door hard behind him just to remind me how pissed he was.

———

A WEEK PASSED.

He didn't text me. He didn't stop by my apartment. He didn't come to my performances.

He disappeared.

I was too stubborn to apologize for it, so I held on to my silence, spent my evenings at home alone, making dinner for myself with the groceries he'd dropped off last time he was there.

But after days came and went, I started to look at my phone more often, expecting him to text me.

He never did.

When the full week came and went, I began to get scared.

What if he'd moved on? What if he'd called Dynasty? What if he'd stopped waiting?

What if I'd lost him?

The fear was so overwhelming that I swallowed my pride and drove over there, not caring that it was almost midnight, terrified he would have another woman at his place when I walked inside.

I didn't park in the garage because I felt like I'd lost that privilege and parked at the curb. I entered the code, relieved he hadn't changed it, and stepped inside his home.

It was quiet.

I took the stairs to the main floor, listening for the sound of the TV, the sound of life. I reached the main room, seeing nothing. The kitchen was untouched, and the living room was vacant. "Heath?" I raised my voice, hoping he wasn't in his bedroom...with a guest.

I heard nothing in response.

I moved into the hallway and stared at his bedroom door. It was wide open. "Heath?"

Nothing.

I turned to the stairway and moved to the third floor. My last hope was he was in his gym, and if not, he just wasn't home. I approached the glass walls and spotted him in front of the mirror, lifting heavy dumbbells as he did his curls.

I closed my eyes in relief, so thankful he was home, thankful he didn't have a visitor watching TV on his couch or lying in his bed. I pushed the door open and stepped inside.

His headphones were on his ears, so he didn't notice me, not until I stepped farther into the room and made a reflection in the mirror on the wall. His eyes flicked to me in the mirror, his arms by his sides as he continued to grip the weights.

He was still, staring at me for several seconds, not the least bit happy to see me.

Was I too late?

He carried the weights to the racks and set them down before he pulled the headphones off his head. "About fucking time." He set his headphones on the bench then loosened his black gloves from his hands. He pulled them off and tossed them on the ground, turning to face me and stare at me in the flesh.

His heart hadn't softened in our separation. He was just as angry as he'd been the day he walked out. He wasn't even impressed by my appearance, by my short dress and heels. He was normally so infatuated with the way I looked that he couldn't keep his hands off me. That attraction had disappeared.

He stared at me coldly, sweat on his forehead and his chest from his workout. "You have something to say to me?" he barked.

God, he was terrifying when he was mad. I came closer to him, my arms over my chest. "I wasn't going to apologize... but then I got scared."

His chest continued to rise and fall from his heavy breathing, from lifting those heavy weights.

"I got scared you would be with someone else..."

He didn't confirm or deny my fear. "This is a shitty apology."

I dropped my gaze, feeling the pain start in my chest and move up my throat. "I know why I reacted that way, and it's just because I was so hurt, so jealous, so...scared. I panicked. I know I overreacted. And it's because of exactly what you said...because of the way I feel about you." I lifted my gaze again, feeling the tears start to burn my eyes.

His expression didn't change—at all.

"I don't know how it happened, but you've become so important to me, giving me a relationship I never thought I would find. I sit in the bar alone and feel so numb...because there's no one else in this world I'd rather be with. I just want to go home and be with you. You protect me. You make me happy. And I just... I can't even stand the idea of you being with someone else—"

"Apologize to me."

I stilled, my watery eyes looking into his.

"You're telling me everything I already know. You think I don't already know how you feel about me? You think I'm at your beck and call because I have nothing else to do? Trust me, I know. I know every time we're together. So, shut up and apologize to me."

I inhaled a deep breath and felt the tears escape. "I'm sorry..."

The second the words were out of my mouth, he dropped his hostility. "I've been home alone, every night, waiting for my fucking phone to ring. And you know that."

I wiped my tears away and sniffled.

A gentle smile came over his lips. "I like it when you get jealous. Means I'm doing something right. Just tone it down a little."

I chuckled through my tears, rolling my eyes at the same time. "You fucking asshole..."

He moved into me, his sweaty arms wrapping around my waist, getting his moisture all over me.

But I didn't care.

His hand slid into my hair, and he brought his face close to mine. "Baby."

I closed my eyes when I heard him say that word, felt his entire presence surround me, protect me.

"Believe me or don't believe me..."

I opened my eyes.

"But I don't even look at anyone else...only you."

FIVE

HEATH

With her back against my mattress, I was between her legs, my arms behind her knees and keeping her legs apart. I rocked my hips and moved deep inside her, feeling her tight cunt squeeze me with a strength that contradicted her size. "Does a man fuck a woman like this if he wants someone else?" Her apology wasn't enough. I was still pissed, furious, that a week of my life had passed without her in it because she took so fucking long.

Her hands cupped my neck, her fingers gliding to my cheeks.

"Answer me."

"No..." She breathed with me, moaned with me, pulled me close like she never wanted to let me go. She'd lost her shit when she saw that message, going back in time like I was trying to kidnap her next to her car. Emotional, fiery, crazy... she lost all sense of reality. And that was all because of me.

"Apologize to me." I rocked into her hard, smacking the headboard against the wall, driving my dick deep inside her to claim her.

She gripped my biceps and dug her nails into my flesh, her tits rocking up and down as I rammed into her. Her lips parted, and she breathed through the explosive pleasure between her legs.

"Now." I wasn't going to let this go easily. I was the kind of man that held grudges—her brother could attest to that.

"I'm sorry..." She spoke against my mouth, one hand cupping my face, her eyes filled with emotional desire. "Babe, I'm sorry." She didn't call me that often, but when she did, it wrapped around me like a collar, like she claimed me in a whole new way.

I slowed down, loving the way she looked, loving the way her hair was all over the place, the way her green eyes were filled with so much, overflowing with thoughts and emotions. She'd stood in front of me and confessed how much I meant to her, that the mere idea of me wanting someone else drove her crazy.

I loved to drive her crazy.

I brought our faces together and thrust inside her slowly, my eyes locked on hers so we could enjoy the steady movement of our bodies. I was still pissed, but when I looked into those green eyes, it was easy to forget her error, easy to forget her tantrum. "You better be."

SHE WAS timid around me for a few days, as if she was embarrassed about the entire thing.

She should be.

I stepped out of the shower and tossed my towel into the hamper in my closet.

She was in bed, scrolling through her phone, buck naked on the sheets because we'd spent the afternoon fucking. When she heard the sound of the towel fall, she lifted her gaze and looked at me, her eyes roaming over my hard body, like she hadn't just gotten my dick for the last few hours. Come seeped from her entrance at that very moment.

I pulled on a new pair of boxers and got into bed beside her.

Now that I was back, her phone was forgotten, and she turned all her attention on me. Her hand moved to my hard stomach as she lay close to me, her hair pulled back from her face, her chin perfectly curved up and away from her neck like a movie director did it that way on purpose. She hadn't put on her makeup, but she was so stunning that way, her olive-toned skin infused with a single freckle.

I'd been with a lot of beautiful women in my lifetime...but none like her.

Her fingers gently stroked my abs, her eyes watching her movements before she looked at me again. Her usual fire was gone. Now she looked slightly uncomfortable, like she didn't know how to behave around me.

"I'm not going anywhere." Her tantrum the other day had only made me want her more, made our passion escalate through the roof. In the moment, I was pissed she would think so little of me, but once I walked away, I realized it had nothing to do with my character. She was just so into me, so possessive of me, that she couldn't control her emotions. It was hot.

She lifted her gaze and looked into my eyes, her fingers stopping. "I know..."

Now I wanted her more than I had before, because being with a woman who was so sprung on me was sexy. Well, not just any woman, but *this* woman. She wasn't going to walk away from me anytime soon. I had her wrapped around my finger—nice and tight.

She grabbed her phone again and looked at the time. "I've got to go." She started to sit up.

I grabbed her wrist and pulled her back. "Go where? You still have a lot of making up to do." A week without sex was insufferable. I went from having the best sex of my life on a nightly basis to being alone, to jerking off to the sight of her panties that she'd left behind. I didn't even like jerking off in the first place. Why would I use my hand when I could have real pussy? "A lot more apologies to make."

She stopped resisting me, letting me hold her wrist all I wanted, but a few months ago, she would have stabbed her fingers into my eyes to get free. "I know, but I have to work." She seemed genuinely sad to leave me, like she wanted to stay there with me forever, like this week apart had been just as difficult for her. "I've got bills to pay."

"I can pay all your bills." The only time I gave a woman money was for sex, but I offered her everything I had for no real reason at all.

She rolled her eyes like she thought I was joking. "I love my job. I mean, I wish I didn't have to go tonight, but...it's fine."

"What would happen if you didn't?"

"My understudy would perform."

"Has that ever happened?"

"No. I always show up. No matter what."

"Well, good to know you have a replacement if I ever decide to tie you up." She probably thought I was joking, but I definitely wasn't. I got out of bed and pulled on my sweatpants so I could walk her to her car in the garage.

She got dressed too, pulling on the outfit she'd worn when she showed up last night. She didn't bring a bag with her, probably because she had no idea where our conversation would go. She was afraid I'd already moved on with another woman.

Who? Who could possibly follow her?

I walked with her downstairs and into the underground garage, where I had my truck and other vehicles. She pressed the button on her keys to unlock her car, but before she opened the door to get inside, she turned to me, her eyes still somber.

"Don't look at me like that." I cupped her face with both of my palms, bringing her face close to mine. My fingers moved under the fall of her hair, cradling her close as I looked into those gorgeous eyes.

"I was so afraid of what I would see when I walked in there the other day..."

She knew how she felt about me, but she clearly had no clue how I felt about her. Maybe she wasn't as smart as I gave her credit for. "No."

She closed her eyes.

"We're gonna fight—a lot. Doesn't mean anything."

She opened her eyes again.

"I said we would fuck the way we fight." My thumb brushed across her bottom lip. "The fighting doesn't stop the fucking." I kissed the corner of her mouth before I released her.

Now her mood had lightened, taking heart in what I said. She finally gave me a soft smile, feeling secure in this relationship once again. She rose on her tiptoes and kissed me on the mouth before she got into the car.

I hit the button on the wall and opened the garage, watching her until she pulled onto the street and disappeared.

I GRABBED a program on my way inside.

Balto didn't own anything remotely nice, so he walked inside wearing jeans and a shirt. When the usher reminded him of the dress code, he slipped him a couple hundred euro to shut his mouth. "I can't believe I'm going to the fucking ballet."

"You want to see my baby, right?"

He shrugged.

I handed him the program. "First page."

He opened it and saw the picture of Catalina along with her description, her other performances as well as a few sentences about her personal life. It was a black-and-white photo, a picture of her side profile, her hair down one shoulder.

I had a program in my nightstand just so I could keep a copy of it.

He scanned it as he walked.

"She's beautiful, isn't she?"

Balto seemed unimpressed, but he nodded. "Yeah." He handed the program back to me.

We walked down the hallway and searched for the aisle to get to our seats.

I glanced in the other direction, for no reason at all, and stilled when I spotted someone familiar.

Damien.

He was with Anna and his father. Dressed in a suit like a prick, he held her hand as he searched for their seats.

Shit.

Then he started to turn my way.

I grabbed Balto by the arm and pulled him behind the pillar.

He moved with me but gave me a cold look. "Got a woman on your tail?"

"I wish." I stayed put and watched Damien take his seat in one of the rows, moving to the opposite side of the theatre. "Damien is here."

"Why does that surprise you?"

I came to her performances all the time, and not once had he shown up.

"You want to go?"

"No." I wasn't gonna walk out just because he was there. I'd rather take my chances. "Let's go." We moved down the aisle and took our seats near the front, squished in the small chairs that weren't made for men our size.

Balto looked bored, like he'd rather be at home with Cassini. "This must be getting serious, then?"

I shrugged. "Might be."

"Then are you going to tell her about your attempted manslaughter?" He turned to look at me.

I stared at the program even though I wasn't really looking at it. The situation with her father hadn't been on my mind because I refused to think about it. I should probably tell her, but that happened before I knew her, so I also felt like it was unfair. "I don't know."

"She'll find out at some point, right?"

I shrugged again. "I'll deal with it later. But for now, I'm just going to enjoy it." The lights were lowered, and the curtain began to open.

Balto continued to stare at me in the darkness, his blue eyes piercing into my face even as the music began.

WHEN THE PERFORMANCE WAS OVER, Balto left and I headed backstage. Now that the girls knew exactly who I was, they didn't hesitate to let me inside to see my girl. I moved through the cast members as they undressed and wiped off their makeup, all moving around the dressing area, congratulating one another.

I saw Catalina sitting at her vanity, pulling all the pins out of her hair so she could get that bun loose and let her long hair fall around her shoulders. Her fingers dug into her scalp and massaged her skull as she closed her eyes and enjoyed it, like that tight bun was uncomfortable throughout the entire performance.

Mesmerized by her actions, I just stared, picturing her doing the same thing in my shower, her eyes closed and her lips slightly parted.

I came up behind her, watching her expression in the mirror.

When she opened her eyes, she noticed me behind her. Instead of giving me a soft smile and looking at me with an affectionate gaze, she looked panicked. She rose from the bench and immediately turned to me. "My family is here. You've got to go."

"I know. I saw them."

Her eyes widened. "Then why are you here?"

"Because I'm gonna kiss my baby and congratulate her." My arm wrapped around her waist, and I kissed her. Once our lips touched, she relaxed, stopped thinking about the possibility of her family catching us together. My hand moved into her loose hair, and I gently rubbed her head, knowing it would make her feel better. The only reason I pulled away was because I had to, because we didn't have the time to make that kiss last.

Her affection immediately died away as she looked past me. "They just walked in. You've got to go. What if they see you?"

I shrugged. "I don't care."

"Well, *I* do care." She pressed her palm against my chest. "Please leave." She glanced at them again, her panic worsening. "Now."

"Alright." I brought her wrist to my lips and kissed her before I moved back. "I'll meet you at the car."

"They're probably going to take me to dinner."

I stopped and turned back to her. "Then I'll meet you at your apartment." I stepped away and walked to the other side of the room, finding cover from a clothes rack on wheels. I didn't have a second longer to linger because they appeared.

Anna hugged her first. "Oh my god, you were so beautiful."

"Thank you." When Catalina pulled away, she forced a smile on her lips, her eyes still giving away her unease if anyone was paying attention. "And thank you for coming."

Damien moved in next, giving her a one-armed hug before he pulled away. "You were great."

"Thanks..."

Her father brought up the rear, holding an arrangement of sunflowers. "Sweetheart, I'm so proud of you." He stared at her like she was his entire world, like the love in his heart couldn't stay inside his chest. "It doesn't matter how many times I watch you, I just can't believe how talented you are."

All the stress disappeared from her voice when she looked at her father. "Thank you, Daddy…"

He gave her the flowers. "Summer is almost over, but I managed to find these."

She took the arrangement from his hands and brought it to her nose so she could smell them. Then her eyes softened in a new way, like the gesture was particularly evocative to her, like it really meant something. "Thank you so much…" She set them in the empty vase on her vanity. When she turned back to him, she wrapped her arms around him and hugged him tightly, closing her eyes.

He hugged her back, cradling her like she was still the little girl he remembered.

Her father adored her, brought her flowers.

I never brought her flowers.

When she pulled away, her eyes were a little wetter than before, like she knew the moment would be a memory that she would hold on to when he was gone. "You guys want to take me out to dinner?"

"Yes," her father said. "And you're going to get a nice tiramisu—and eat it all."

The joy I felt from kissing her was long gone. Now I felt pain, unbearable agony. I'd made a mistake I could never take back, did something unforgivable. Seeing how close she was to her father shattered all my hopes.

She would never forgive me for what I did. We couldn't work past it. Time wouldn't heal the wound.

Once she knew, she would leave me.

And never come back.

MY CLOTHES WERE on her bedroom floor, and I lay against her headboard in my boxers. The blinds to her window were open, so I stared at the buildings across the street, one hand behind my head as I replayed their interaction over and over in my head.

If only I could go back in time.

The locks to the front door clicked open, and Catalina stepped inside.

I was just about to get up to greet her when I heard other footsteps accompanying her. I settled back onto the bed and became still so they wouldn't hear my large size make the bed creak.

"You guys didn't have to walk me all the way to my door." Catalina's purse made a distinct thud on the counter when she set it down. Then her keys rang as they clattered against the dish in her entryway.

Damien's deep voice was filled with concern when he spoke. "Cat, what's with your door?"

She played dumb. "What do you mean?"

"It's got five bolts on it, and it's not the door you had before." Suspicion was pregnant in his voice, picking up on the details only a criminal would notice. "And you have an alarm. Cat, what's going on? You aren't telling me something."

I listened for her response, wondering how she would handle this. She probably knew I was in her bedroom, listening to the entire exchange.

"There was a break-in a few weeks ago," she said. "My neighbors told me about it, so I asked my super to get a better door. That's all. And the alarm is just good sense." Her footsteps sounded as she walked across the floor. "Who wants wine? I just got a few new bottles the other day."

No, I did.

"I'll take some," Anna said.

Damien didn't let it go. "If you don't feel comfortable here, I can always buy you a place—"

"Oh my god," she said with a scoff. "Don't be a drama queen. Now, you want red or white?"

Damien backed off, grudgingly. "Red."

"Me too," Anna said.

"Daddy?" Catalina asked, her voice a higher pitch whenever she spoke to him.

"I guess red," he said, his voice deep and raspy.

She poured the glasses and handed them out. It seemed like Damien and Anna moved to the living room because their voices were farther away. Her father started to speak to her, keeping his voice down like he didn't want his son to overhear.

"Maybe your brother is right," he said, his voice coarse with age. "He could buy you a nice place close to the theater—"

"Daddy, I'm fine," she said quickly. "It's not his responsibility to take care of me. He has someone in his life he's supposed to care for, and that's exactly how it should be. I'm not his problem."

"Sweetheart, we're a family. We always take care of one another."

"I'm perfectly fine, okay? One day, I'll have a man who can take care of me the way Damien takes care of Anna."

That could be me...if she let me.

"I don't believe that," he said. "Because I can't imagine any man being good enough for you."

There was a long pause, like she was taking it in. "Daddy..."

"I mean it. Who's ever gonna be good enough for the smartest, most talented, most beautiful woman in the world?"

"Stop," she said with a chuckle. "And even if that's true, it doesn't matter. I'm perfectly capable of taking care of myself."

Her father was quiet for a while. "Sweetheart, I'm glad you're a dancer because I can't imagine you doing anything else, not when you're so talented, but it'll never earn you enough money to be comfortable. Your brother has enough money to share with you."

"Dad, just let it go, okay?" she said gently. "I'm only twenty-five. I've got time to worry about that stuff later."

"Alright," he said. "I just want to make sure my little girl is taken care of."

I sighed to myself, hated listening to this conversation, listening to the bond they shared. He was a sweet old man who loved his daughter so much, wore his heart on his sleeve, and after what I did... I was fucking evil.

They all chatted together on the couch for another fifteen minutes before they decided to leave. It was getting late, so I was surprised they'd stuck around so long. The front door opened, and they said their goodbyes.

"Goodnight, sweetheart. Come over tomorrow so we can play a round."

"Alright, Dad." She kissed him, probably on the cheek. "I'll see you at lunchtime."

"I love you, sweetheart."

"Love you too, Daddy."

I pushed my fingers through my short hair and down the back of my neck, sighing to myself.

Anna said goodbye next. "Let me know when you want to go out to lunch. Sofia is having her baby any day now, so I won't have long lunches anymore."

"Alright, girl," she said.

Footsteps sounded as they stepped into the hallway.

That meant Damien was the only one who stayed behind.

"Oh no..." Catalina sighed. "Not you too."

"Let me buy you a place," he insisted. "It doesn't have to be fancy."

"I don't need you to buy me anything, Damien."

"Then move in with me. Come on, there's plenty of space for all of us."

She released a sarcastic laugh. "God, I'd rather be homeless than live with you, Damien."

He chuckled slightly in return. "It wouldn't be that bad. We'd set some ground rules to make it work."

"Yeah?" she asked sarcastically. "What about when I want to bring..." She faltered for a moment, choosing her words carefully before blurting them out. "My guys over?"

He sighed loudly. "We're both adults, Catalina. I understand you have a personal life. I wouldn't say a word."

"You would hate it, and you know it."

"But I would keep my mouth shut."

She turned quiet. "I appreciate you looking out for me, but I'm fine. Really. Don't worry about me."

"You're my little sister. Hard not to."

"I'm not *little*, Damien."

He chuckled. "Let me know if you change your mind. Offer is always on the table."

"I know."

Their voices shifted like they shared an embrace.

"And you were amazing tonight, by the way."

"Thank you."

He walked out and shut the door behind him.

I stared out the window and listened to their footsteps fade down the hallway. Catalina didn't move, probably staring at the door to make sure they were really gone before she turned all the bolts into place.

Then her footsteps came my way.

I turned to the door, expecting to see her any second.

She came inside and looked at me, not the least bit surprised to see me lying on her bed. Her eyes scanned me over, noticing my nakedness. "What if they'd walked in here?"

I shrugged. "If they saw me in your bedroom, they would know we're fucking, so I didn't see why it mattered."

"You could have closed the door."

"Would have made it obvious you were hiding something."

She didn't lean down to kiss me, probably because she was still anxious about the whole thing. "Want some wine?"

"Sure."

She walked back into the kitchen.

It gave me time to clear my thoughts, to stop thinking about what I'd just heard, to stop thinking about the future and just live in the moment. I got out of bed and followed her, seeing her stand at the kitchen island and pour an extra glass.

I stood across from her at the kitchen island and grabbed it, taking a deep drink.

She did the same, swirling it when she was finished then taking another sip. When she set it down, her eyes moved to her glass, her thick lashes covering a small part of her cheeks.

"You're close with your father." I'd never wondered about her relationship with her family. When I was with her, I only saw her, not the people she was connected to. She was just mine…and that was all that mattered.

"Yes. I'm his favorite."

"No surprise there."

She smiled slightly and lifted her gaze. "It's not because I'm better than Damien."

"I disagree."

She ignored the jab. "It's because I look just like my mother." She swirled her glass again and took a drink. "He says I keep her spirit alive, that all he has to do is look at me when he misses her…and it feels like she's still here."

I watched her face, mesmerized by all the subtle expressions she made, how beautiful she was when she was sad. "Then she must have been gorgeous."

She looked at me again, a slight smile on her lips. "She was."

I took a deep breath as I stared at her, so deeply transfixed by her appearance, I felt paralyzed. I couldn't look away, not even to grab my glass, because she'd never looked more beautiful than she did in that moment. My eyes burned as I looked at her because my stare was so rigid. I could feel the tightness in my face because I'd held the same expression so long. But whenever I looked at her, that was all I could do... look. "How did she pass away?"

"She got sick." She turned away and opened one of the drawers until she found a stack of pictures. Then she came back to me, sorting through the pictures until she found one she liked. She held it out to me.

I took the picture and stared at it, staring at a brunette with the same green eyes. She sat on the beach with Damien playing with his toys beside her. She seemed to be the same age Catalina was now—and the resemblance was uncanny. "You weren't kidding." I handed the picture back to her.

"No." She flipped through more pictures until she found one that had all four of them. She and Damien were just small children.

I didn't care about Damien or the other members of her family. I stared at her, the little girl with a big bow in her hair. A smile came onto my lips before I returned the picture.

She returned it to the stack before leaving it on the counter. "Our family was never the same after she was gone. My father stopped smiling. He hasn't smiled the way he used to since she was alive. He always tells Damien and me we need to have children, that we shouldn't wait until we're older like he did, because we'll have less time with our kids...and that's his biggest regret in life."

I never thought about having kids. I was willing to get married if it happened, but having kids...not so sure. Balto was going to do it, and I was curious to see how that would go.

"My father has been attached to me ever since. I know he loves Damien, but I comfort him in a way Damien can't. Damien has her eyes, but that's about it. The rest of his genetic inheritance comes directly from my father."

That explained her exceptional beauty and his plainness. "I'm sorry you lost her."

She opened the drawer and returned the pictures before she came back to me. "Thank you."

I hated to see her sad, but her eyes had a special quality that was so breathtaking. It was like looking at the nighttime sky and seeing nothing but bright stars.

"What about you?" she asked. "You don't talk about your family."

Because there was nothing to say. "My father beat my mother repeatedly and ultimately disappeared. She died of her injuries. My brother and I made our own way in life."

She watched me, unable to hide her surprise at my tale.

"Don't feel bad for me. I turned out fine." I never cared about not having a family because I had Balto, and that was more than enough. Our lives were different from everyone else's because we got involved in crime to survive. Anyone outside of our background and profession could never possibly understand.

"Never said you didn't."

"Well, you're looking at me like you feel sorry for me."

"No," she whispered. "I just think you deserved better, that's all."

"That's not how life works. You don't *deserve* anything." Everything I had was a result of hard work and a high tolerance for risk. My life was on the line many times, but I never had anything to lose, so I wasn't gambling much in the first place. But now I was at the top of the food chain, with more money than I could spend, with a beautiful woman who wanted me all to herself. Now I had everything to lose...and it was fucking scary.

She watched me for a while, her green eyes still soft and vulnerable. It was a side to her she didn't show often, but the longer we were together, the more she displayed it. She was less afraid to be weak, less afraid to show me her scars.

And that made her irresistible.

She grabbed her glass and finished it off. "Keep an open mind, alright?" She cleared her throat.

My eyes narrowed on her face.

"What if I just tell Damien the truth?" She released the deep breath she'd been holding. "He respects me, so he'll listen to me. He'll do anything for me...anything."

My heart started to race because that was the worst thing she could possibly do. If she told him about me, he would tell her what I did...and then it would be over. There was zero chance it wouldn't come up in their conversation, and there was zero chance Damien would ever let my crime go. "That's the worst thing you can do. There's nothing you could possibly say to make him feel differently about me." If she knew the truth, she wouldn't even entertain the idea. But then again, if she knew the truth, we wouldn't be together that very instant. "I've tried to bury the hatchet with him before. I've given him chances to let this go. He won't."

Her eyes filled with disappointment. "Maybe you could try harder—"

"There's not much more I can do."

"But there's something."

I could stop collecting payment altogether, but I'd have to hide the truth from my men, and Damien would definitely be suspicious. "If I stop collecting, he'll know something is up. He's not stupid."

"I don't know... He can be pretty dumb."

I smiled slightly. "Just let it go, baby." We should enjoy this time together until it was over. It would be over someday, so we should spend every moment together like it might be our last...because it could be our last. The end of the relationship wouldn't even be the most painful part. It would be her reaction, the way her affection would quickly turn to hatred with the snap of her fingers.

She stared at her empty glass and didn't say more about it.

At least that was over. "Are sunflowers your favorite?"

She took a few seconds to raise her chin and look at me again. "Yes."

It was an interesting choice, but it fit her well.

"Summer is my favorite season, and that's the only time of year they grow so..." She shrugged. "We're kind of the same in that regard. I hate it when it's cold. I'll continue to wear dresses through November because I just refuse to let the season end." She chuckled to herself. "I'm weird like that."

I'd just learned something new about her, and that new information made her so much more desirable. We'd met at the beginning of summer, and now it was almost over. I never knew her in any other climate.

"What about you?"

I raised an eyebrow, unsure what the question meant.

"You have a favorite season?"

"No. But I like it when it's cold."

She stuck out her tongue as she grimaced. "Ugh, I hate winter."

"I run hot, so you might feel differently about it this year." I could keep her warm every single night, keep her warm anytime she wanted me inside her. She could wear my sweaters and jackets, could move into my side and suck all the warmth from my skin whenever she wanted.

She shrugged. "We'll see..." She pulled the bottle of wine toward her and refilled her glass.

I watched her pour it, watched her carry herself with such poise.

"Why do you keep staring at me like that?" She grabbed my glass and did the same, not lifting her gaze as she asked the question.

"Do I need a reason?"

"No." She lifted her gaze and took a drink. "But I'm curious."

Sometimes I thought my thoughts were written across my face, like a billboard on my forehead. But maybe my expressions weren't as decipherable as I thought they were. "Because I think you're beautiful."

She held her glass and held my look, her eyes searching into mine.

"It's what I always think...every time I look at you."

SIX

CATALINA

When the performance was over, Tracy came to my station. "We're going out to dinner for Nina's birthday. You in?"

Going out for a meal sounded like more fun than going to a bar. "Will there be birthday cake?"

"Yes."

"Then count me in."

"Excellent." She clapped her hands excitedly then walked off. "Cat's in."

I removed my stage makeup and touched up with the makeup I'd brought from home, so I wouldn't look like a prostitute when we were at the restaurant.

"Catalina." Andre came up behind me, wearing a collared shirt tucked into his dark jeans with a dark blazer.

"Hey. What did you think?"

He clapped his palms together, his chin covered in a shadow and his eyes brown like chocolate. "Perfect, as always."

"Good. I give it my all every night."

"Yeah, I can tell." He was the director of the production, in charge of every theatrical performance we did. He was a brilliant man, able to create a story without words. "I was gonna see if you wanted to get dinner."

Andre and I had fooled around in the past, a short-term fling we didn't really talk about. I'd never told anyone about it, and I doubted he had either. He was a handsome man, and his gifts made him more attractive. I wasn't sure if that was where he wanted this conversation to go, but I gave him the benefit of the doubt. "We're going out for Nina's birthday."

"Oh, yeah," he said with a nod. "You guys have fun."

"Thanks." I turned back to the mirror.

"Maybe we can go out another night."

I sank into my chair, feeling the tension settle over my shoulders. I remembered how angry I got when Heath had women hit him up for sex, that he didn't tell them he was in a relationship. So, I had to do the same, even if he would never know about it. "I'm seeing someone, actually." I rose and faced him again.

He didn't hide his disappointment. "Yeah, the girls mentioned him. I didn't think it was serious."

It wasn't serious, but it was...something. "Yeah, it is." I didn't know how long it would last, but I didn't want to keep Andre on my hook.

He nodded slightly. "Well...he's a lucky guy." He turned around and walked off.

We hadn't hooked up in a long time, so a part of me wondered if he only wanted me because I was unavailable. That seemed childish, especially for him since he was almost ten years older than me, but he was also artistic, emotional, spontaneous...a lot like me. "Thanks."

———

WE HAD DINNER, cut the birthday cake, and after a few hours of having a good time, everyone started to file out and go home. I walked out with Tracy.

"You didn't bring your man?" she asked.

"No. It's nice hanging out with you guys without him all over me."

"Really?" she asked, walking with me out of the bar. "You seem pretty miserable when he's not there."

"At the bar, yes. There's nothing for me to do while you guys get laid."

"Hmm...I guess that makes sense."

"But when we go out to dinner, we're just hanging out, so it's fun." I got to spend time with just them, not having to worry about guys sending us drinks and taking all their attention.

"Well, we'll make more time to do things like that since he's not going anywhere."

I hoped he never went anywhere. I'd just stepped out of the door when I realized what I'd forgotten. "Ugh, I'm so stupid. I forgot my purse."

"You want me to wait for you?"

"No, girl." I rolled my eyes. "I'm parked the opposite way anyway."

"Alright. See you later." She kissed me on the cheek.

"Bye." I headed back inside and reached the table that the busser was cleaning. It hung over the back of my chair, out of sight, which was how I'd forgotten it in the first place. I grabbed it and headed out again.

But stopped when I saw Heath.

He sat at a table with a beautiful brunette, their hands together on the surface. With striking blue eyes, he stared at the woman like she was the only thing that mattered... exactly the way he looked at me.

What the fuck?

I looked at his hands, seeing the sleeves of his shirt reach his wrists, and just below that was the skull ring he always wore, glittering in the candlelight.

I was frozen to the spot, unable to believe this was real.

It couldn't be real.

He would really do this to me...after everything that already happened?

The waiter brought the bill, and Heath reached into his pocket and grabbed a wad of cash before he slipped it inside the tab. Then he and the woman rose from their seats and headed to the main doors, his arm around her waist.

Then he grabbed her ass.

The same emotions that hit me in my bedroom rushed back to me, suffocating me, drowning me. The betrayal was like a knife to the throat, cutting my windpipe so blood flooded my airway.

Heath told me I was wrong, even made me apologize for it, and then he did this shit?

Tears burned in my eyes because I was devastated.

Fucking devastated.

I should just leave and cut him off from my life, block his phone number and change apartments so I could get rid of him for good. But taking the high road was never my style, so I went after him, ready to release my wrath.

I pushed through the double doors and watched them walk down the sidewalk, his arm still around her waist.

"Hey, asshole." I walked fast in my heels, as if I were wearing flats.

He didn't turn around.

"I'm talking to you, piece of shit!"

He halted and slowly turned around, his blue eyes narrowing on my face like he was annoyed.

Fucking prick.

Instead of slapping him like I always did, I did something worse. I pulled my elbow back and punched him hard in the face, getting a clean shot to his cheek that actually made him step back because he hadn't been expecting it.

He groaned and stumbled back, his hand on his cheek as he looked at me incredulously.

I could kill him right now. "I can't believe I bought a word you said. I can't believe you had the audacity to tell me to trust you when you're a lying, worthless asshole." I moved toward him again.

The brunette stepped in front of him. "Touch my husband again and see what happens."

Heath placed his hand over her stomach and gently pushed her back, moving forward so she was behind him.

My hand slowly lowered, my breathing more labored, my eyes stinging with painful tears. "Husband?" How was I so stupid? How did I not see any of this? How did Heath hide everything from me without giving me any clue?

He raised his hand, as if he was ready to catch my fist if it launched at him again. "I'm not who you think I am, Catalina." He lowered his hand. "I'm Balto...Heath's brother."

I had no idea why I laughed, but I did. "How stupid do you think I am? I know I shouldn't have believed you before, that's on me, but I'm not gonna fall for this bullshit." I pointed at his hand. "You think someone else has the exact same ring as you do?"

"Yes." He spoke calmly. "Because there are three. I have two, and Heath has one."

I rolled my eyes. "Be a man and be straight with me. Don't hide behind these lies. It's so fucking insulting—"

He suddenly pulled his shirt over his head and extended his entire arm out to me.

That shut me up.

"Heath and I are twins. I guess he didn't tell you that."

I stared at his naked arm, seeing nothing but skin and muscle. There wasn't a single tattoo anywhere, not on his stomach or chest either. "Oh my god…" I was relieved that this wasn't real, that it was just a mistake, but I was also more mortified than I'd ever been. "Oh my god…" I covered my face with my hands, unable to handle this horrific reality. I'd just punched his brother in the face and unleashed insult after insult. "I'm so sorry." I lowered my hands and looked at his bruised face, knowing that was going to be worse in the morning.

He stared at me with the same cold expression his brother gave, his intense gaze impossible to read.

When he told Heath what I did, Heath would be pissed at me again…because I didn't trust him like I said I would. I assaulted his brother and caused a scene on the sidewalk, ruined any chance for him to ever like me. "I'm so sorry…" I turned around and walked away even though my car was in their direction. I was so mortified, I'd rather round the corner and wait for them to leave before going back to my car.

When I turned the corner, I leaned against the wall with my head against the bricks, drowning in self-loathing.

When Balto told Heath what I did, it would be bad. Heath assured me that fights were just fights, that they didn't mean anything, but I suspected this would be different.

Oh god.

SEVEN

HEATH

Balto stood in front of the liquor cabinet in his living room, pulling the doors to reveal a stash of booze big enough to last until the apocalypse. Since he wasn't drinking as much as he used to, his stockpiles probably didn't deplete at their normal rate. "What do you want?"

"Vodka."

"Just vodka?" he asked incredulously, pouring himself a drink.

"Yeah. With a splash of another kind of vodka." I took a seat on the couch, glancing at the TV.

Balto turned around with the drinks in his hand and moved to the couch beside mine.

I stared at his face, my eyebrow immediately rising to the ceiling. "What the fuck happened to you?" His entire right cheek was discolored like a huge guy punched him so hard he'd cracked Balto's cheekbone.

He slid the glass toward me before he took a drink of his own. "Glad you asked..." He took a deep drink before he returned it to the coaster. "Why didn't you tell Catalina we're twins?" He rested his arms on his knees as he stared me down, clearly annoyed with me.

The question caught me off guard. "What does that have to do with anything?"

He pointed at his face. "Because *she* did this to me."

I stared at him blankly, unable to process what I'd heard.

Cassini emerged from the kitchen, wearing jean shorts and a t-shirt that showed her small pregnant belly. She had a plate of snacks and set them down on the table. "Balto and I were out having dinner, and she saw us walk out."

I stared at her, imagining Catalina's horror when she saw me with someone else, and knowing my brother, he'd probably groped his wife in public. Catalina had to see that and assume I was a pathological liar.

"She came after my husband hard," Cassini said. "And when I told her he was my husband...the look on her face." After the food was on the table, she sat on Balto's knee, her arm wrapping around his shoulder.

Balto secured his arm around her waist. "I explained who I was, but she didn't believe me." He raised his hand. "Because of this. Heath, she lost her shit, exploded like a volcano. So, I took off my shirt and showed her my bare arm and chest so she would see I had no tattoos. She finally backed off."

I dragged my hands down my face, finding the situation obnoxious and hilarious. "Jesus..."

"She apologized then took off," Balto finished. Now he stared at me, the same way his wife stared at me, like I owed them some kind of explanation.

I dropped my hands and released a quiet sigh. "I told her I had a brother, but I guess I forgot to mention that other part..."

Balto rolled his eyes. "That's not something you just forget."

"Well, I did, alright?" I grabbed the snacks off the dish and placed them on a plate, eating like nothing happened.

Balto raised an eyebrow. "Is the conversation over?"

"What do you want me to say?" I countered. "It's not like Cassini got the wrong idea about everything."

"I know my husband would never fool around, so that was the last thing on my mind," Cassini said. "I was just worried she might stab him or something. She was furious."

"Devastated," Balto said. "Truly, deeply, devastated."

I continued to eat, trying not to imagine the scene.

"Tears," Cassini said. "Heartbreak. Insults. It was a fucking soap opera."

"You want me to apologize?" I asked incredulously. "Look, I'm sorry I didn't tell her I had a twin. My bad."

"No," Balto said. "I just want you to know how attached this woman is to you. You said it wasn't serious, but it's pretty fucking serious. You should have seen her face, Heath. And I've had ice on this injury for two days, and I still look like shit."

"This happened two days ago?" I asked in surprise.

Balto nodded. "She didn't mention it?"

I shook my head.

"She's probably embarrassed," Cassini said. "It definitely wasn't her finest moment."

I put the plate down and finally addressed the situation. "Yeah...she's crazy about me." I grinned like an asshole, giving a slight shrug. "She saw a text from one of my girls a few nights ago and lost it. So, this is a subject we've already dealt with recently. I guess I'm not surprised."

"And it looks like you're crazy about her," Balto said.

I didn't bother to deny it. "A bit."

Cassini smiled slightly. "So...what does that mean?"

"It doesn't mean anything. I'll enjoy her until it's over." I chose to live in the moment, not think about the painful day when my world would crumble around me.

"Why does it have to be over?" Balto asked. "Come clean about what happened, then give her some space."

I shook my head. "No. It'll never work."

Balto raised an eyebrow.

"I've seen her with her father...they're really close. They have that father-daughter relationship you see in family movies. You know, ridiculous and cheesy." I bowed my head. "Once she knows the truth, she'll leave me. And worse, she'll hate me. So, no, I'm not gonna tell her. The second I do, it's over. So, I'd rather just wait until the shit hits the fan on its own. Yeah, that makes me an asshole for not being honest with her, for letting her sleep with me when she wouldn't if she knew the truth...but I don't care. I had no idea our relationship would escalate into this, so it wasn't that premeditated."

Balto didn't argue with me, perfectly understanding my reasoning. "I'm sorry."

Knowing exactly how it would end made it less painful, because I already anticipated it. But for Catalina...it would be sudden, horrifying, and completely unexpected. Or maybe we would be together for a long time, a secret relationship that would last years since she didn't need a husband until she turned thirty. Then I wouldn't have to worry about it for a long time. "I'm sorry about everything that happened. I understand if you don't like her now."

"Don't like her?" Balto asked, his deep voice filled with surprise. "Why would I not like her?"

I tapped my finger against my cheek. "Because she turned your face into a pinata."

He glared at me.

"We didn't like what was happening at the time," Cassini said. "But we can't blame her for making the wrong assumption since you didn't give her all the facts. And the fact that she cared so much...tears down her face...did make me like her. Because she obviously adores you, Heath."

Balto rubbed his cheek. "And I like any woman who can throw a punch like that. Impressive."

"Yeah..." I smiled slightly. "She's feisty."

"She chased me down on the street and handed my ass to me in less than a minute. Sounds like the perfect woman, if you ask me." My brother was a no-nonsense kind of man, so he respected people who were the same way. Instead of being annoyed or intimidated by a woman who spoke her mind and put her fist where her mouth was, he found it endearing, which was obvious, considering Cassini was the same way. I'd never forget the time she hit me in the face with a fucking lamp.

I chuckled. "Man, I wish I could have seen that."

"It wasn't funny—at the time," Cassini said. "I don't appreciate someone striking my husband."

"Baby, I'm fine," Balto said quickly. "And I've had worse." He turned back to me. "The four of us could have dinner and break the ice."

"You want to go on a double date with me?" I asked incredulously.

"Why not?" Balto asked. "This woman is obviously special to you. And you dragged me to the goddamn ballet. At least at dinner, I can eat and drink. I can grab my wife's ass too."

Cassini smacked his shoulder playfully.

Balto grinned slightly, like he liked it when she hit him.

I liked it when Catalina hit me too. "I'll talk to her about it when I see her." It would be an interesting conversation, to say the least. After our explosive argument over those dirty pictures, our relationship had taken a brief, steep nosedive. "I'm not sure what she'll say about dinner."

"Don't give her a choice," Balto said. "You think Cassini gets a choice in anything?"

She smacked him again then got off his lap. "I get a choice in serving you dinner." She headed back into the kitchen. "Looks like it'll just be me and Heath. Enjoy your scotch."

———

I LET myself into her apartment.

She stood at the kitchen counter, her back to me. Without turning around to see my face, she addressed me. "Hey, babe. Just finishing dinner." She wore her sexy little shorts and a tank top, skipping the bra and letting her tits relax. Her ass cheeks hung out slightly because the bottoms were so short.

Babe. It was a title I'd never been called before, and it fit me like a tailored suit. I liked listening to it come from her lips, especially since she only did it once in a while, when she really felt the affection inside her heart. Every time she said it, she meant it, and that was sexy. "What are we having?"

"Spaghetti." She sautéed the beef in the pan while the noodles boiled in the pot.

I came up behind her, my arms wrapping around her petite frame, covering her entire torso because our sizes were so vastly different. I pulled her into me slightly, my face moving into her neck so I could kiss her, placing my lips against that delicious skin.

She immediately froze when I kissed her, holding the spatula over the pan without stirring the food.

I pushed the strap off her shoulder so my kiss could migrate down, move across the rest of her tanned skin, tasting olives on my tongue. My mouth widened and kissed her harder, my dick pressing into her back because I held her close. My fingers gripped the thin fabric of her shirt, stretching out the fibers with my aggressive clenches. I kissed her shoulder like it was her mouth, sucking, licking, biting.

She abandoned the food entirely, closing her eyes as she felt me devour her.

My hands roamed all over her body, squeezing her tits through the shirt before moving across her stomach. My lips slid back to her neck, and I nibbled on her lobe before I let my warm breath enter directly into her ear so she could hear my pants. I gave her a final squeeze before I let her go. I stepped over to the cabinets and grabbed the plates along with the silverware. I knew she liked wine with dinner, so I grabbed a new bottle and uncorked it.

It took her a few seconds to snap out of her haze, to stir the meat before it began to burn. But there was a red tint to her cheeks like her mind immediately went to the gutter, like food was the last thing she wanted to eat.

I leaned against the counter and stared at her.

She stirred the meat again before she looked at me. She held the look for a few seconds before she continued what she was doing.

"So, you met my brother."

She dropped the spatula onto the pan, her relaxed body now tightening in distress. She quickly grabbed it before it became too hot to touch. The food seemed to be done, so she turned off the burner and wouldn't look at me.

I waited for a response.

She opened a cabinet and grabbed a strainer before setting it in the sink. Then she grabbed the pot and dropped the water and noodles into the metal strainer, steam rising and filling the kitchen, floating past her face and toward the ceiling. Her arms shook the bowl, letting the water drip out.

"I asked you a question."

She finished straining the noodles before dumping everything back into the pot. Then she carried it back to the stove. "You didn't ask me anything."

I smiled slightly at her comeback.

She spooned the meat onto the noodles then added the sauce, stirring everything together before she added a splash of oregano and garlic. Then she sprinkled Parmesan cheese on top. When she had nothing else to do, she sighed. "Look, I didn't know you had a twin." She finally turned and faced me, unable to hide the fear in her eyes. She was actually afraid of my reaction. "You guys are the same weight, the same build, and he had a skull ring. You can't blame me for making the assumption. And...I'm sorry that I punched him. I apologized to him—twice." It was the first time she was unsure of herself, showing her embarrassment. "It doesn't mean I don't trust you, okay? It just—"

"Baby, I'm not mad at you." I couldn't stop the smile from entering my lips. "But I do enjoy watching you squirm."

Her eyes flashed with her usual fire.

"Why didn't you tell me?"

"Because...I'm embarrassed." She scooped the meal onto the plates, averting her gaze so she wouldn't have to look at me.

"I guess I didn't want to deal with this conversation until I absolutely had to."

I knew that feeling too well.

"How does his face look?"

"Like a busted pinata."

"God…" She carried the plates to the table and sank into her chair, covering her face with both hands.

I took the seat beside her and grabbed her wrist, gently pulling it away from her face. "Come on, you're too beautiful to hide your face."

She dropped her other hand and sighed. "They hate me, don't they?"

"No. Actually, the contrary." I grabbed my fork and started to eat.

She turned to me, visibly surprised. "They don't?"

I shook my head as I chewed. "My brother is not your typical guy. He was impressed by your punch."

"What?" she asked incredulously.

"And his wife understood after the fact. I told them I didn't tell you I had a twin."

"Why didn't you?" she asked.

I shrugged. "Didn't think you'd bump into him on the street."

She grabbed her fork and started to eat.

I watched her face as I ate, loving the way she struggled with her humiliation, the way she wore her heart on her sleeve, tears in her eyes. "They told me you were devastated when you thought I was married."

She spun her fork around and collected a portion of the noodles. "So?"

"That you were completely and utterly devastated."

"Who wouldn't be?"

"A woman who doesn't care. But you clearly do."

She continued to spin her fork even though all the noodles were securely wrapped around the utensil.

My hand moved to her wrist, my fingers giving her a light squeeze.

She sighed in defiance.

"Baby, look at me."

She refused.

Maybe she wasn't just humiliated about what she did to my brother. Maybe she was humiliated by the way she felt about me, the way she allowed me to pierce her heart and every other inch of her body.

She finally turned to me, the shame still in her eyes.

I interlocked our fingers and continued to stare at her, to look into those gorgeous green eyes and see her thoughts written with bright ink. "I'd be just as devastated..."

I SAT on the couch in my living room and watched the game while she sat on the other end of the couch, reading a book. Summer had faded quicker than normal, fall coming quick and sudden, so she wore my t-shirt and my sweatpants, the fire in the hearth burning to keep her warm.

I was pretty much naked and totally fine.

She grabbed her phone and checked the time before she sighed. "I should get going." She closed the book and left it on the coffee table. Her things had been gradually left at my house, extra clothes, her books, some heels. They were left in random places, on my nightstand, in my drawer, in my closet, etc.

I pulled my gaze away from the game. "Why?" It was getting late in the evening, and I knew she didn't have a performance on a Wednesday night. I tried not to demand explanations from her because she never did it to me, but this time, I couldn't help it.

She rose from the couch. "I have a dinner to go to."

"Dinner?" I asked, wondering if it was a girls' night.

"Yeah." She placed her hands on her hips. "The entire ballet is going to this charity dinner at the Tuscan Rose. So, I need to head home and get ready." As if she hadn't said anything worth discussing, she walked down the hallway to the bedroom.

I watched her go, the muscles in my arms tightening in annoyance. It only took me a few seconds before I followed her, telling myself to tone down my anger before I even spoke. I stepped into the bedroom and watched her return her essentials to her bag. "You better be fucking joking." My attempt to control my anger was unsuccessful—extremely. But I was a candid man who spoke his mind, especially to the woman who had prime real estate in my bed.

She stilled at my words, her eyes widening at my outburst. "What?"

"Don't *what* me," I snapped. "You have an event to go to, and you didn't think to ask me."

She shoved her heels inside and sighed. "It's black tie. You don't wear stuff like that—"

"But I have the ability to buy it."

"Well, there's no time now—"

"Because you purposely waited until the last minute."

She stopped packing and stared at me.

"Why don't you want me to come with you?"

She shed her clothes and put on the jeans and shirt she'd left out. "It's not really your thing. This is a fancy event. You don't know how to act or talk to people."

My eyes narrowed. "You think I'm stupid?"

"That's not what I said—"

"It's what you're implying. And trust me, I can handle a few pretentious assholes in suits. You should see the other shit I handle on a nightly basis."

She left my clothes on the bed and shouldered her bag. "Heath—"

"Baby." I came farther into the room, my eyes burning into her face. "I'm your man. You don't go to shit alone when you have a man. How would you feel if I went somewhere and pretended I didn't have a woman at home?"

"I don't pretend you don't exist, Heath. I just thought—"

"Stop thinking on my behalf. I don't need a woman to speak for me, to make my decisions. This is a relationship, whether you fucking like it or not, and you will treat me with the respect I command."

She crossed her arms over her chest and slightly tilted her chin down.

"What? Are you ashamed of me?"

"No." The answer burst from her lips immediately, like it was an instinct.

"Then what the fuck?"

"I just..." She looked away as she ran her fingers through her hair. "I don't know. I've never been in a relationship before, and this wasn't even supposed to be a relationship, and now I'm having to do things I've never done before. I've never brought a man to anything before."

"How is it any different from us together at the bar?"

"Because those are just my friends. This is with other people I work with, other people in society. A lot of people know my brother, and they might mention this to him."

"So?" I asked. "You aren't scared to tell him off, so if he sticks his nose in your business, tell him to fuck off."

She sighed quietly.

"If you really don't want me there, then fine." I turned away, swallowing my pride and dropping the conversation. I wasn't going to beg her to take me, to make her do something she didn't want to do. I had too much self-respect for that shit.

"Heath."

I kept walking.

She came after me and grabbed me by the arm. "Wait."

I only turned around because I wanted to, because whenever she touched me, I turned into a fucking pussy. I looked down at her, my eyes still full of rage.

"I'm sorry." Her hands grabbed onto my arms, her chin tilted up so she could look into my gaze. "It's not that I don't want you there. It's not that I'm ashamed of you. It's not that I'm trying to hide you. I guess I like my independence, and I have to learn to let that go…because I'm not alone anymore. I have you."

I stared into her eyes and saw her sincerity.

"I'm just not used to being two people…instead of one."

When we met, she told me all these things, that she didn't want to settle down for many years. This was supposed to be a fling, one which probably should have burned out by now, but it turned into something neither one of us expected. "Then ask me to come with you."

She smiled slightly once I forgave her. "Come with me."

The brightness in her eyes allowed me to believe her, allowed me to let it go. "Don't let it happen again." I would give her a pass on this, but she better learn from her mistake, better not pull this stunt again.

"I won't."

I cupped her face and leaned down to kiss her. "Alright." I released her and walked back into the bedroom.

She followed behind me. "It's black tie, so what are you going to do?"

I pulled on a shirt and grabbed my jeans from the closet. "Go to Balto's."

She cocked an eyebrow, not following my thought process.

"We're the same size—so his suit will fit me."

"Does he even own a suit?"

"One." I came back to her and pulled on my shoes. "The one he wore on his wedding day."

CATALINA WAS STUNNING.

She wore a backless dress, falling so deep down her backside that the top of her ass was nearly visible. Her hair was pinned around her head, wrapping all the way until her long strands fell down a single shoulder. With dark makeup on her eyes and sparkly jewelry, she looked unbelievable.

Thank fucking god she didn't come alone.

My arm was around her waist as we walked inside, collecting the flutes of champagne offered to us.

This suit was stuffy, the tie like a rope around my neck. My temperature always ran hot, so I felt twenty degrees hotter than usual. I'd picked up a fifty-thousand-euro watch on the way home just to wear for the evening, even though I never wore jewelry except the ring on my hand. I felt ridiculous in the outfit, like a goddamn clown.

But Catalina couldn't stop looking at me—like she liked it. It was the same look she gave me when we were in bed together, that she couldn't believe just how sexy I was, that she couldn't handle my cut physique, that she couldn't believe I was real.

So that made it worthwhile.

Her friends stared at me too—a lot.

She introduced me to a few people, and she was initially surprised at how well I could handle myself, shake hands with strangers and make small talk, even make people laugh. The longer the night went on, the more impressed she became.

When we had a minute alone together, she turned to me, her eyes almost level with mine because of the sky-high heels on her feet, adding at least five inches of height to her petite size. "You look really good in that suit..." She looked me up and down as she drank from her glass, smearing her red lipstick against the edge.

I knew she was used to seeing powerful men dressed that way, like her brother and Hades. I took the compliment without issuing a comeback. "Not as good as you do in that dress." If this event weren't important to her, I would take her into a bathroom and fuck her in a stall.

She smiled slightly, her eyes playful.

"I can't wait to see how that suit looks on my bedroom floor."

I cocked my head slightly, enjoying the way she objectified me. My arm circled her waist, and my hand pressed into her bare back, my fingers digging into the muscles surrounding her spine. I pulled her into me and kissed her, the kiss a little inappropriate for the setting, but she didn't pull away.

She liked it.

I ended the kiss and kept my forehead against hers, loving it when she was this height. I knew men liked their woman short, but I liked it when she was elevated, when I could look her in the eye without bending my neck down. In general, I preferred taller women because of my height, but all Catalina had to do was pull on heels to meet that requirement. And during sex, it didn't matter what her height was.

She cleared her throat and pulled away, knowing the affection would only escalate if she didn't end it before it got out of hand. She brought the glass to her lips and downed the rest of it.

"Want another?" I took it from her fingertips.

"If you don't mind."

"I never mind." I also wanted something stronger from the bar because this bubbly shit was lame.

She grabbed my wrist to stop me before I left. "I have to say, I had no idea you could be a gentleman."

I came back to her, leaning in close. "I can be anything. I just choose not to be." I kissed her on the cheek before I walked away. I glanced at her friends as they stood together near the bar, watching us like we were their favorite soap opera on TV. With looks of longing in their eyes, they seemed like they wanted exactly what we had.

That meant I did my job right.

I got to the bar and ordered my drink.

When I turned to look at Catalina, she wasn't alone. Someone quickly swooped in to speak to her the instant she wasn't preoccupied with me. He was slightly shorter than me, good-looking, and seemed to be a few years older than me. He wore a dark blue suit, his hands in his pockets as he spoke to her. But I didn't like the way he stared at her.

It was the way I stared at her.

I grew impatient as I waited for my drink, wanting to return to my woman so I could chase off this dog.

But she continued to talk to him like she knew him well, like he wasn't some random guy making a pass at her. He came closer to her and continued to speak, his hands staying in his pocket, but his proximity was inappropriate.

I could read people well. I did it for a living. And I didn't like what I was reading.

Her arms were crossed over her chest, her body language showing her mood.

The drinks were finally given to me, and I returned, ready to knock this guy's teeth out in front of everyone he knew.

The guy glanced at me, a subtle reaction of unease coming over his face as if he wanted to avoid me.

Too fucking late.

I returned to her and handed her the champagne. "Baby." I didn't need to call her that because I wasn't addressing her at all, but I blanketed her in my affection before I wrapped my arm around her waist and turned to the asshole who wouldn't stop staring at my woman. I stared him down in silence, refusing to extend my hand and introduce myself. I didn't give a shit who he was. I didn't fucking like him.

And I wanted him to know that.

When Catalina realized my best behavior was long gone, she cleared her throat. "Andre, this is Heath..."

I was irritated she didn't give me a more detailed introduction. "Her man." I extended my hand.

He didn't match my intensity, immediately cowering once he was confronted by a man who could kill him with a single punch. He shook my hand. "Nice to meet you."

Catalina was clearly annoyed with my reaction, but she tried to hide it. "Heath is the man I told you about." She seemed to say that just for me, so I would understand she wasn't playing games or hiding my existence from people she knew.

Smart choice.

"Andre is my director. We've been working together for a few years." When she looked at me, she gave me a fiery look, warning me not to do something stupid and piss off her boss.

Like I gave a damn. "I've seen the show many times. A masterpiece." I didn't give a damn about the dancers or the music. All I cared about was the beautiful brunette surrounded by my arm that very moment, owning that stage like she could do the entire show on her own.

He nodded. "Thank you. Catalina is definitely my star." He stepped back. "Enjoy your evening."

I watched him walk away, bringing my glass to my lips for a drink to wash away my rage.

When we were alone, she turned to me. "What the hell was that?"

I lowered my glass and turned to her, my eyebrow raised. "I could ask you the same thing."

Her eyebrows furrowed at the question.

"You slept with him, didn't you?"

Now, her eyes were wide. "Why would you assume that?"

I came closer to her, keeping my voice low. "Answer the question."

She took a deep breath, visibly irritated to be put on the spot. "Yes."

I already knew her answer before she gave it, but it sent me into a rage anyway. When a waiter with a tray passed, I set my drink down because no amount of alcohol would tame the monster bursting from inside my chest.

"What does it matter?"

"You slept with your director?" I asked incredulously. "Your fucking boss?"

Her flames started to match mine. "You sleep with prosti-tutes, but that crosses the line?"

"He's way older than you."

"Oh, and you aren't?" she hissed.

I really wanted to rip that fucker's head off right now. "Not by a decade. He completely took advantage of you—"

"Advantage?" Her voice started to rise, indifferent to the people who might be able to hear us. "I'm not a little girl. I'm a grown-ass woman who was attracted to an older man. I fucked him, and I liked it. Alright?"

My hands tightened into fists because I wanted to kill that motherfucker. I wanted to throw him out the large windows and watch his body drop to the concrete five floors below. "That was the reason you didn't want me to come tonight." I turned back to her and stared at her, finding the answer I'd been searching for.

She didn't deny the claim.

"Because he still wants to fuck you, and you knew I would figure it out."

"I certainly didn't figure out you would behave like this. You say I'm jealous?" She pressed her hand into her chest. "When he came on to me, I told him I was in a serious rela-tionship with you, which is more than you said to Dynasty or whatever the fuck her name is."

My eyes shifted back and forth quickly, the pulse pounding in my neck and temples. "Not the same thing at all, and you know it. Maybe if you had some sense and didn't fuck every guy you see, you would have known better than to screw your own boss." The instant the words were out of my mouth, I knew I'd taken it too far. I knew I'd fucked up—bad. I didn't mean a word of it, but I said it just to hurt her—which was worse than if I meant it.

Her expression didn't change, her eyes open and glued to my face, but her breathing picked up, like she was so angry, she didn't know what to do, didn't know how to respond to the insult I'd just shoved in her face. "Wow...didn't know you were a misogynistic, toxic hypocrite." She would probably slap me if the room weren't full of people. She turned around to storm off, but she only made it a few steps before she turned around and came back to me. "No, I'm not going to leave. *You're* going to leave." She pressed her hand hard into my chest. "Get the fuck out of my sight. Pack up my shit and leave it in my apartment—and leave your key too." She turned around and walked off, moving into the crowd and grabbing a glass of champagne on the way. Then she walked right up to Andre and engaged him in conversation.

Just to piss me off.

———

I LEANED against the wall in the hallway, my hands in my pockets as I stared at the painting across from me, reflecting on that terrible conversation that got out of control so fucking fast.

It was a goddamn tornado. It started as a breeze, but within seconds, it destroyed everything in its path, turning into a whirlwind that destroyed entire towns, destroyed people's lives.

I leaned my head against the wall and closed my eyes, hating myself for the way I'd handled it. She didn't want to bring me because she feared I would behave exactly how she assumed I would behave.

And I proved her right.

I didn't want to embarrass her even more by hunting her down and pulling her away from her conversation, so I waited in the hallway, hoping she would use the bathroom or leave at some point.

Then the sound of heels hit my ears.

She stepped out of the double doors and walked into the hallway, so oblivious to everything around her that she didn't even notice me standing there. She headed for the bathroom, sniffling.

"Baby." I moved behind her.

She halted, jumping at the sound of my voice. She clearly thought I'd already left, had no idea she would bump into me again. She took a few seconds to turn around, and when she did, her gaze was so hard, it seemed as if she hadn't been on the verge of tears to begin with. "Get the fuck out of my face—"

"We fuck the way we fight—and we fight the way we fuck." I came closer to her, pulling my hands out of my pockets.

"If you think we're gonna—"

"I'm sorry."

She shut up, breathing loudly.

"That was a really fucked-up thing to say. I didn't mean it."

She rolled her eyes. "You've made enough comments to indicate otherwise—"

"And I didn't mean those either."

"Then why would you say them?" She crossed her arms over her chest.

I was quiet for a while as I considered my answer. "You want to know the reason I let you go?"

Her hostility immediately dropped because she hadn't expected me to say that. Her eyes narrowed in confusion.

"Because I heard you pray. I heard everything you said. I heard you say you've slept with more guys than you should have..."

She was still, waiting for more.

"I know you're insecure about it, so I used it against you...to hurt you. But that's fucking worse than meaning it, and I'm sorry." I rubbed the back of my neck, my other hand sliding into my pocket. "I don't understand why I got so upset about Andre. I don't understand why I hate the idea of you being in a bar alone. I don't understand why every guy before me bothers me so much. I've been in denial, but it's fucking obvious, staring me in the goddamn face." I looked away for a few seconds before I met her gaze again. "I'm jealous..."

She took a deep breath.

"Out of my fucking mind, inexplicably, insanely jealous." I dropped my hand and felt the humiliation wash over me.

She stared at me for a while, her eyes hiding her thoughts so clearly. "You told me to trust you, but it doesn't seem like you trust me."

"I do." I said the words without thinking. "I'm not worried about you being with someone else. Andre is nothing compared to me. Why would you want another man when I'm one of a kind?"

She dropped her gaze.

"That's not what upsets me. It's..." I shook my head. "It's possessiveness. It's jealousy. It's emotions I can't even comprehend. I've never felt this way before. I've never had a woman I didn't want to share."

She lifted her gaze again. "I know exactly how that feels..."

It was fun to watch when I was on the other side of the conversation. But being the culprit was no fun at all. My flesh had been stripped away, and there was nothing but my feelings underneath—and she could see them all. I couldn't hide them anymore. "I'm sorry. I couldn't care less where you've been, how many guys you've slept with, because there's nothing wrong with it. Your past doesn't matter. Only your present does—with me."

She watched me for a while. "I've never been with a man who makes me feel the way you do...because you are one of a kind. My friends aren't just jealous of me for having you. They're jealous because of the way you look at me, the way you treat me. They're jealous of everything that we have. I don't look at other men because there's nothing to look at. You're it..." She didn't need to say any of that because her feelings were obvious in everything she did, from losing her mind with jealousy to fucking me nonstop throughout the night.

I smiled slightly, relieved that she forgave me, that she wanted me enough to excuse the shitty things I said.

"But you need to trust me..." She stepped closer to me, her arms loosening from across her chest and moving to my biceps. She tilted her gaze up slightly to look at me, staring through her thick eyelashes. "Do you trust me?"

My arms moved around her body, my hands planting against the bare skin of her back. My fingers dug in slightly as I pulled her closer, bringing our faces close together, my eyes looking into hers with a new kind of intensity. "With my life."

EIGHT

CATALINA

THE CLOTHES CAME OFF THE SECOND WE GOT HOME, the pieces of his suit like breadcrumbs down the hallway. His watch came loose and landed somewhere on the bed, and my small black dress was hanging on the bedpost.

With his powerful arms behind my knees, he took me deep and slow, his mouth kissing mine as he rocked into me over and over. With every thrust, he pressed deep within me, getting his entire cock inside before he pulled out again, his lips never breaking with mine.

My nails scratched down his back, marking his skin with my long nails. I kissed him back, but it became harder and harder as my body prepared to explode. "Come inside me..." I spoke against his lips, opening my eyes so I could see his eyes staring back at me. We had just begun, and he usually waited for me to come at least once before he released, but I was too anxious. "I want to feel it while you fuck me." His seed always dripped between my legs and got on his sheets, acting as the lubricant between our already wet bodies.

He moaned against my mouth when he heard my request, aroused by the demand. He pumped into me a few more times before he released, groaning loud against my mouth as he stuffed my pussy with every drop of his seed. He paused as he finished, breathing against my mouth as he felt the shiver in every nerve of his body. Then he started to move again.

I pulled him close and kissed him again. "That's better…" It didn't take me long to reach my own climax, to come around his dick the way he'd just come inside me. I sheathed him with a flood of moisture, our bodies mutually soaked for each other.

He watched my face as I came around his dick, watching my performance while he continued to slam his fat dick inside me, his come and mine dripping down my crack to the sheets underneath us.

I could do this forever.

I never wanted this to end, this unbelievable passion to die away. There would never be another man to make me feel like this, to take my breath away with just a kiss. When I was old and gray, I would remember these nights with a blush in my cheeks and a smile on my face. It would be something I thought about when I was alone with my vibrator in the years to come. It would be something I'd think about when I slept with my husband, even though I'd try so hard not to let the memories flash in my mind.

But they would.

I didn't want to think about the expiration date on this relationship, not when it gave me everything I hadn't known I needed. I had no idea men like him existed, that they were this strong, that they were this good in bed.

Or was he the only one?

We moved together until we were both finished, our earlier fight erased from our minds. It was like it never happened, like it didn't matter, and why would it when we had this? Our wet bodies came to a gradual halt, and I cupped his face as I kissed him, so satisfied but insatiable at the same time.

He slowly pulled his dick out of me before he rolled over, his heavy body collapsing on the sheets, his skin coated in his sweat. One arm moved under his head, and he looked at the ceiling for a few seconds before he closed his eyes.

I did the same, letting my body cool off, letting his come drip from between my legs. I noticed every time I came over, his sheets were clean and fresh, so I assumed he or someone else was washing them several times a week. I had to do the same to my own.

I turned on my side and looked at him.

He seemed to feel my stare, because he opened his eyes and turned his head my way, a sleepy look in his gaze.

"You said you listened to me pray...and that was why you let me go."

He kept his same stoic expression, one hand on his stomach.

"What did you mean by that?"

He turned to the ceiling again, as if he was thinking about the question before he gave an answer. He sighed and turned over, facing me with the sheets up to his waist.

"People only pray when they want something. You wanted something—but not for yourself."

I couldn't remember what I said word for word. In that moment, I had been afraid I'd end up stuffed in an oil drum.

"You didn't ask God to save you. You asked him to protect your brother—and spare your father any pain. It was the first time I'd ever heard someone be so selfless, think about someone else when their life was hanging in the balance." His blue eyes were vulnerable and open, letting me see all the way to his soul. "I've never heard anything like it."

"And that made you want to let me go?"

He nodded.

"But wasn't that part of Liam's plan? How did that work?"

"I gave him a better suggestion so I could let you go."

So, this man really did save my life—and my brother's.

"I told him to fight Damien face-to-face in the ring. Then, you were no longer needed."

"All because of the words I said to the big man upstairs?"

He nodded.

Unsure what to say to that, I just stared, stared at this beautiful man. I'd thought about my time in his cage many times, wondered why this man released me when my odds of survival seemed too slim. That felt like a different time now, even though it was just a few months ago. And this man felt like a whole different person.

"Do you have to work tomorrow?"

His question brought me back to the conversation. "No."

"You want to have dinner with me?"

"I always have dinner with you." We were together almost every single night, sleeping over at each other's places in an unpredictable pattern. We usually cooked something at home and watched TV on the couch. Our nighttime routine was to go to bed, have sex, and then fall asleep.

"I mean go out to dinner with me."

"Oh...sure." I didn't mind going out to a restaurant with him, but to be honest, I preferred eating at home. When we were out, I couldn't touch him the way I wanted, couldn't say whatever popped into my mind because it was too inappropriate for a public place.

"Balto and his wife will be joining us too." He smiled slightly, as if he anticipated my tantrum before it even happened.

"Wow...back up."

He chuckled.

"What do you mean, they'll be joining us?"

"As in, they'll be sitting at the same table as us, sharing an appetizer with us."

"Why?"

"Because it's rude not to share."

I slapped his arm because now wasn't the time to be a smartass.

He chuckled at my venom. "It was their idea."

"Because Cassini wants to fight me?"

Now, he laughed. "No. And if she did, you would kick her ass, baby."

I was still mortified by that night. I wouldn't be able to look them in the eye ever again.

"Come on, it's not a big deal."

"Uh, you weren't there. I slugged your brother like I was a bully on the playground."

"And I wish I had been there. Would love to see my woman kick my brother's ass."

I glared at him. "This isn't funny."

"I don't know…"

I smacked his arm again.

"Baby, there's nothing to be embarrassed about. They don't dislike you."

I covered my face with my hands. "Ugh…"

He grabbed both of my wrists and pulled them from my face. "I thought my baby wasn't afraid of anything?"

"I'm not…except humiliation."

He brought my wrists to his lips and kissed each one. "Come on."

"Why do we have to have dinner at all?"

He shrugged. "My brother wants to meet you—properly. He's my closest friend, so it makes sense that he wants to spend time with the woman I'm seeing."

This was supposed to be a fling, not a relationship where we met each other's family.

He seemed to read my thoughts. "I've met your friends."

"But you haven't slapped any of them..."

"On the ass, maybe."

My eyes turned to fire.

He smiled, telling me it was a joke. "You and Cassini will get along well."

"Uh, I really doubt it." I remembered the way she threatened me when I struck her husband.

His arm wrapped around my waist, and he pulled me close. "I know you're embarrassed, but I think it's a lot more embarrassing not to show up. Then they'll think you're weak, that you don't have the spine to look them in the eye, have the balls to keep your confidence, have the poise to laugh it off like the funny story it is."

Damn, he got me. "Alright..."

———

HE PARKED his truck at the curb and turned off the engine.

I looked through the windows at the tables inside the restaurant. It was a busy night, the tables full of couples and families. I could feel his stare against the side of my face. "This is gonna be weird."

"Only weird if you make it weird."

I turned back to him, seeing the outline of his pecs in his shirt. He was so muscular and firm that the clothes he wore couldn't hide how fit and sexy he was. It left little to the imagination, but when he was naked, it was so sexy. "I meant because you're twins. There will be two of you..."

"My brother and I are nothing alike."

"Really? Because he grabs his wife's ass exactly the way you grab mine."

He grinned. "Baby, that's just a man thing." He opened the door and got out.

I joined him on the sidewalk, and we entered the restaurant. Heath wrapped his arm around my waist and guided me to the table, seeming to know exactly where his brother was sitting.

We approached the table, seeing Balto with his arm around his wife's shoulders, looking at her like he didn't hear a word she spoke, just watched her lips move because he was utterly infatuated with her.

I got that same look from Heath all the time, and now that I saw it from an objective view, I realized just how potent it was, how lucky I was that I had a man who looked at me like that. I was jealous of their affection even though I already had that chemistry with someone.

Heath cleared his throat and pulled out the chair for me. "Make out later, alright?"

Now that I was face-to-face with them again, the nerves got to me. My heart raced so fast, and I felt so out of place, not my usual confident state.

Heath sat beside me, his arm moving over the back of my hair just the way Balto's did with his wife.

Balto slowly turned his gaze to his brother, his blue eyes just a tad bit more hostile than Heath's usually were. "Would you rather me kick your ass instead?"

Heath grabbed the arancini balls from the center of the table and dropped them on his plate before he ate one whole. "I'm too hungry right now." He placed one on my plate. "These are good, baby. Try one."

He just called me baby in front of his family, and I was too nervous to enjoy it. I sliced my fork into the rice ball and took a small bite. "Yeah, they are good." I put the fork down and stared at them both, the memory of that night fresh in my mind. "So...I'm super sorry about that night—"

"Don't apologize." Balto cut me off with his deep voice, sounding just like Heath. His face was still slightly bruised, but he'd healed pretty well. "Honestly, when you did that, I knew you were perfect for my brother."

"Did Heath tell you about the first time we met?" Cassini looked at me, her long dark hair that was almost black, with almond-shaped eyes and a beautiful smile. She had a glass of water in front of her while Balto had a scotch.

"No." I ate the rest of the rice ball on my plate. "What happened?"

Heath chuckled. "I was an asshole, basically."

"Or should I not tell it?" Cassini asked. "Don't want to throw you under the bus in front of your girl."

Heath shook his head. "I have nothing to hide. Catalina knows my dirtiest secrets, and she still wants to be with me..." He turned his gaze on me, wearing a slight smile. "So, I think she can handle it."

When he looked at me like that, I knew I could handle anything. Those eyes...that smile...the thick chords in his neck. He was the sexiest man in the world...and he was all mine. I turned back to Cassini.

Balto was still staring at his brother, wearing a serious expression.

"Alright," Cassini said. "He was living with us at the time and stopped by, pretending to be Balto. We shared a few words and then—"

"She smashed a lamp over my head," Heath finished. "And pointed a gun at me."

I turned to him, both of my eyebrows raised. "What?"

"Yep," Heath said. "Look at us now, we're brother and sister. So, if we can get past that, you guys can get over this."

I turned back to Cassini, seeing her smile at me.

Balto continued to stare at his brother.

When the waiter came over, Heath ordered a bottle of my favorite wine for us to share.

He didn't even need to ask.

"Barsetti Vineyards?" Balto asked, his eyebrow raised.

Heath shook his head. "Leave it alone."

"What's wrong with Barsetti Vineyards?" I asked, catching on to their tone.

Balto gave a slight shrug. "Don't have a problem with the wine. Just the family."

"It's a long story," Heath said. "But the Skull Kings and the Barsettis don't mix. We're like oil and water."

The waiter brought the wine, uncorked it, and poured our glasses.

"But I'm willing to put aside our differences for you." Heath clinked his glass against mine. "You guys ready to order?"

"I'm always hungry." Cassini placed her hand on her stomach. "Well, we both are."

Now I looked at her with new eyes. "You're pregnant?"

She nodded as she continued to rub her stomach.

"Oh my god." I turned to Heath. "That means you're going to be an uncle."

"A terrible uncle," Heath said with a chuckle.

Balto ordered. "I'll take the tenderloin—well done."

"No." Cassini grabbed his menu. "He'll have the salmon. I'll have the garden salad with chicken." She handed the menu over and gave him an annoyed expression. "We agreed you would cut back on the red meat."

Balto turned to his brother, his nostrils flaring slightly. "Alright, baby."

Heath found it entertaining; it was obvious by the way he smiled. "I'll have the tenderloin—just to be an asshole." He handed over the menu.

Balto lifted his glass to his lips and whispered. "Fucking bastard..."

"Sorry, did you say something?" Heath asked. "I don't speak pussy."

Balto slammed his glass down.

Cassini grabbed his arm and gave it a gentle squeeze. "Chill."

I didn't laugh, but the exchange between the two men was comical. "I'll have the soup and salad. I'd like to add salmon to my salad, please." I handed over the menu and watched him walk away.

"You're the one ordering Barsetti wine," Balto grumbled. "You're the biggest pussy here..."

Cassini slapped his wrist. "None of that. We're having a good time."

"A good time?" Balto asked incredulously. "Heath is being a dickface." He turned to me. "Why don't you punch him in the face like you did to me? Then you and I will be even."

Heath turned to me, a little smug. "That would be pretty hot."

Balto rolled his eyes and drank from his glass.

Heath moved his hand to my thigh under the table, giving my bare skin a gentle squeeze. Then he leaned in and rubbed his nose against mine, not afraid to show me the same affection he showed me behind closed doors, not being a different person just because we were out in public. He was the same man, just a little more relaxed now that he was with his family.

When he pulled away, I looked at his family again.

Cassini was watching us, a slight smile on her lips. "You guys are both pussies. Just leave it at that."

Heath leaned into me and kissed the corner of my mouth. "If this is what it's like to be a pussy, I don't mind it." After he held my gaze for a few seconds, he faced forward again, grabbing his glass and taking a drink.

I had to force myself not to stare at him, to think about the other people at the table. I thought it would be awkward after what happened on the sidewalk, but now that the ice had been broken, it felt right. "Do you know what you're having?"

"A boy," Balto answered. "A little man."

"Aww, that's so sweet," I said. "Got a name picked out?"

"No," Cassini said. "No idea. But we've got time."

"Heath is pretty nice…"

Balto gave him a cold look. "I would never do that to my son."

"Oh, shut up," Heath responded. "I'm gonna pretend to be you all the time and teach him shady things."

"I'll kill you," he snapped.

"Or I'll kill you and pretend to be his dad forever." He shrugged and swirled his wine.

"Baby." Balto turned to his wife. "This was a terrible idea."

She patted his arm. "He's just teasing you."

"Or am I?" Heath shrugged. "Cassini and I would be great together—"

Balto grabbed his steak knife even though he wouldn't use it for dinner. "I'll slit your fucking throat." It was clearly a joke, but that didn't matter to him.

"Balto." Cassini pulled the knife out of his hand and put it on her side of the table. "Your brother likes to get under your skin, and you're making it so easy for him to do that." She rubbed his arm to calm him down.

Heath turned to me, a slight smile on his lips. "This is fun."

Damien and I teased each other, but we never took it this far. It was a side to Heath I was unfamiliar with. He was playful, sarcastic, funny. He wasn't just the intense man that I knew best.

"Anyway…" Cassini turned to me. "Tell us about yourself."

"Where did you learn to punch like that?" Balto asked, grabbing his scotch and taking a deep drink.

"This guy I used to date a few years ago." He taught me everything I knew, and he was right, it probably saved my life.

Heath didn't react to my comment even though it probably annoyed him. After our last fight, he knew he had to work on things as much as I did.

"And I'm a dancer—for the ballet."

"You're very talented," Balto said.

I raised an eyebrow. "Have you come to the show?"

He nodded to his brother. "Heath dragged me along a couple weeks ago. Not really my thing, but he wanted me to see you dance."

I turned to Heath, surprised he would bring his family along.

"I wanted to show off how hot you were." His hand moved to my shoulder and gave me a gentle squeeze, leaning close to me to show me the affection in his eyes.

"For the record, I do not think you're hot." Balto raised his hand and looked at his wife. "Heath is just trying to throw me under the bus."

"You don't think I'm hot?" I asked, pretending to be hurt.

Heath immediately caught on to what I was doing and grinned.

Balto faltered at the question. "Uh..."

"You think I'm ugly?" I asked, pouting my lips.

"No, that's not what I said," Balto said quickly. "You're very beautiful. I just—"

"Excuse me?" Cassini snapped, playing along. "Did you just check out another woman while your pregnant wife is sitting right here?"

Balto looked away and sighed before he grabbed his scotch and took a drink. "Fuck all of you."

SUMMER HEAT HUNG on by a thread, about to slip through my fingers and disappear for nine months. The nights started to get cold, and while I continued to wear dresses, I paid for it dearly.

We said goodbye on the curb of the sidewalk, their truck somewhere farther down the road.

Heath kept his arm around me, trying to keep me warm.

"Thanks for dinner," Balto said. "But it was the least you could do after being an ass all night."

Heath shrugged. "It's the least I could do since I'm the richer one."

Balto narrowed his eyes. "Fuck off, Heath."

"Ooh...did I strike a chord?" The taunts never ended.

Cassini reached out and shook my hand. "It's nice to formally meet you—on much better terms."

I laughed. "Thanks for giving me another chance. And, again, sorry about before..."

"Don't worry about it," she said. "It's a funny story we'll tell years down the road."

I stared at her blankly as I focused on what she'd said, the implication of her words. Did that mean she and Balto expected me to be around for a long time? Or was that something Heath had said to them? Or was I simply reading too much into it?

Balto extended his hand to me next. "It was nice to see you again."

I gave him a firm grasp and nodded. "You too."

He pulled away and tapped his fingers against his cheek. "Keep up the good work. More women need to know how to throw a punch." He turned to his brother next and didn't show him physical affection before he turned away. "Night, asshole."

"Night, bitch."

As Balto walked away with his arm around his wife, he raised his hand and flipped him off.

Heath called out after him, "Love you too." He turned to me next and wrapped his arm around my waist before he walked me to the truck. "My place or yours?"

Seeing the way he interacted with his brother made me adore him more, for reasons I couldn't explain. It humanized him, showed a playful side I'd never met before. It was sexy. "Yours."

"You got it." He opened the door for me.

I eyed the gesture in surprise.

"What?" he asked. "I can be a gentleman."

I smiled before I got inside.

He drove us to his place, pulling into the underground garage before we entered his fortress.

I walked to his bedroom, my stomach stretching out my dress because I had way too much to eat. Those glasses of wine along with the bread and appetizers filled my stomach because I was distracted by the good conversation. "I liked your brother and sister-in-law."

"Cassini is great. Balto..." He pulled his shirt over his head then removed his jeans. "He's a drama queen."

I chuckled. "I know you don't really think that."

"I do think he's a bitch."

"You don't think that either." I turned to him, unzipping the back of my dress so it could peel off my body and fall to the floor.

He sat on the edge of the bed in his boxers, his back perfectly straight because he carried himself with such discipline. His eyes immediately glanced over my body, seeing me standing in my bra and panties. He didn't argue with me, choosing to stare at me and let the conversation die.

I stepped into his closet and opened one of his drawers, pulling out a silver handgun. I came back to him, pointing it toward the ceiling.

He watched me. "What are you doing, baby?"

"You said you would get me a gun and show me how to use it." I moved to the spot beside him and sat down, aiming the gun at the opposite wall.

"I remember. But now that you have me, I don't see why you need a gun."

"You never know." I shrugged.

He took the gun from my hand. "Alright." He turned it on its side. "You see this black button? Slide it to the right when you want to release the safety. Do it."

I took it from him and repeated his movements.

"Now, turn it back on."

I slid the button back into place.

He took the gun back from me and yanked on the barrel so the gun opened, showing the bullets inside. "You just drop your bullets there to load it. I'll give you some before you leave tomorrow." He closed the gun again then placed it in my hand, positioning my fingers so I gripped the gun correctly. "Your forefinger goes here. Then you squeeze the trigger. Safety is on, so go ahead."

I pulled the trigger, but nothing happened.

"And that's about it. You can keep this gun since you picked it out." He took the gun from my hand and placed it on his nightstand.

"You don't want to teach me to aim?"

He turned to me, his blue eyes on mine. "Baby, if someone really threatens you, I know you won't miss." His arm moved around my waist, and he pulled me close, his head resting on mine. "But nothing is going to happen. I give you my word."

I pressed my cheek against his shoulder, loving the warm heat against my skin. "No one would try to hurt me because you're seeing me?"

He released me and looked down at me. "I don't talk about my personal life at work."

"So, no one knows I exist?"

"One of my guys, but that's it." He spotted the disappointment in my gaze. "It's not because I want it to be that way. I just think it's best if people know as little about my life as possible. Not everyone underneath me wants me to be the leader."

"Really?" He was a strong, hard man. He was honest and fair. And he could be terrifying without even raising his voice.

"If everyone likes you, that means you aren't making tough decisions. And if you aren't making tough decisions..." He shrugged. "Then you aren't the leader the Skull Kings need."

His words reminded me of the conversation Damien had with Hades, a detail I'd forgotten about because it wasn't relevant at the time. "When I overheard Damien and Hades talking, they mentioned something else..."

Heath watched me, deadly serious. His playful mood had evaporated, and it was all business now.

"I can't remember exactly what Damien said, but Hades said if he took you out, the Skull Kings would hunt him down, but he said he made a deal with someone so that wouldn't happen...Fox? Box? I can't remember what he said. It was a weird name, and he said it right as Hades was leaving."

Heath didn't react overtly, but his entire body subtly tightened, his blue eyes focusing on a more intense level, like those names meant something to him. "Vox."

"Yes. Something like he would take your place..."

He stared right into my eyes, but he didn't seem to be seeing at all. Now, he was a different man, immune to my nearly naked body, no longer living in the same reality as I was. Seconds passed before he abruptly left the bed and walked into his closet.

"Heath?"

He ignored me as he got dressed. He pulled on jeans and a long-sleeved shirt before placing a black leather jacket on top, clearly intending to be outside in the cold tonight. He came back out, shoving a gun into the back of his jeans.

"I'm sorry I didn't mention it before—"

"I have to go." He left the bedroom and walked down the hallway.

I didn't have time to get dressed, so I followed after him in my underwear. "Heath, what's happening?"

He reached the stairs that led to the basement, but he stopped to look at me. "I've got to take care of something. Go home. I have no idea when I'll be back."

"What's happening?"

"One of my own plotted against me. I'm going to put a bullet in his fucking head." His expression was tight, the veins noticeable on his forehead and neck. His size had increased, like an animal on the defense.

"I'm sorry I didn't tell you sooner. I'm sorry I forgot—"

"You don't owe me an apology." He turned to the stairs.

I grabbed him by the arm. "Wait."

He didn't come back, but he didn't keep walking.

"Are you going to be alright?"

He pulled his arm out of my grasp. "I'll be fine."

"But..."

He kept walking. "I'll call you when it's finished." He reached the landing and looked up at me. "Don't call me. I'll be busy." Then he walked out and left me alone in his house. Our fun night had been ruined. A part of me wished I hadn't said anything, but a bigger part of me wished I'd told him sooner.

NINE

HEATH

When all that shit had gone down, all I'd cared about was the phone call.

The moment Catalina betrayed her family to save my life.

I didn't think about Damien's intentions, how he would navigate life once I'd been killed. I just assumed that he was too impulsive to think about the repercussions of my death, that he wanted me to pay for what I did, regardless of the consequences that would follow.

But now I knew the truth.

Vox.

He'd plotted against me, took advantage of the opportunity to take my place on the throne. He didn't necessarily plan my execution, but he was disloyal by not telling me about it.

I descended to the Underground and couldn't believe my luck when I found Vox sitting there, chatting with his cronies by the fire with a woman on his lap. Their mugs of newly brewed beer were in front of them.

I pulled out my gun and shot him in the arm, carefully avoiding the innocent bartender on his lap.

Every man in that room cowered down once the gunshot rang out, their heads snapping in my direction as I walked across the room.

The woman screamed and ran away, blood all over her bare tits.

Vox cupped his arm with his palm and grimaced, refusing to let out a scream even though a bullet had pierced his arm all the way through.

His men stilled, watching him then watching me, unsure what was going to happen.

I made my way to him, taking my time as the silence surrounded us, as the fire made the only noise in the room. I walked up to him, seeing him staring at me with fury, looking past those thick eyebrows as he panted through the pain, the blood dripping down his arm. "Tell them what you did." I raised the gun and pointed it at his head.

He was silent, refusing to cooperate.

"Then I'll tell them." I lowered the gun. "You plotted to overthrow me. When Damien took me out, you intended to take my seat on the throne. You know that's a crime punishable by death."

He didn't rise from his seat on the bench, continuing to his grip his arm to stop the bleeding. He kept his mouth shut, refusing to beg for his life, refusing to admit he did anything wrong.

All the men stared, unsure what would happen.

I'd already shot one of my men and that had cost me popularity points, plus Vox was one of the better Skull Kings, in terms of enforcing laws and collecting payments. So, I had a better idea to punish him, one that would work out for me and heighten the opinion of the men underneath me. "So, this is what we're going to do." I moved past him and walked up the steps to the wall behind my throne. I pulled out the blade from my pocket and approached the wall.

The Wall of Traitors.

A few names were already there, carved into the wall even though those people were long gone, but the memories of them were forever tainted by the inscription. I slammed the tip of my knife into the wall and took my time, making sure the cuts were deep, that they would never fade in time.

V.

The men were so quiet, I could hear the knife slice into the wood.

O.

If Vox could pull out a gun and shoot me, he would. But he was outnumbered by all the men who were loyal to me.

X.

I sheathed my knife and turned back to him. "You're forever known as a traitor—and traitors can never be king." I snapped my fingers. "Get your ass up here."

He stared at me from his seat, his look venomous.

Steel rose from a different table and wrapped his arm around Vox's neck. "The Skull King just gave you a command." He dragged him off the bench and onto the floor. "Get your ass up." He kicked him hard in the side.

Vox moaned as he continued to grip his arm.

The humiliation must have been overwhelming, to feel all your comrades look down on you like you were garbage.

He finally pushed himself up and stared at me.

I snapped my fingers. "I'll shoot you again."

He finally moved, walking up the steps as he gripped his wound.

I yanked his hand free of his shoulder and slammed it against the wall, making his blood smear across his name, fill the crevices so the stain would dry and last forever, so all the Skull Kings could see it every goddamn day.

When the deed was done, I released him. "I now pronounce you a traitor. You'll live as a traitor. And you'll die as a traitor."

WHEN I PULLED into the garage, her car was still there.

I'd told her to go home.

I entered my house and took the stairs to the second floor.

She must have heard my arrival because she ran to the top of the stairs, relief moving into her eyes when she saw me, saw that I was unharmed, that I was in one piece. "Thank god..."

I reached the top level and walked past her. "I told you to go home." I turned my back on her and grabbed a bottle of vodka before I filled my glass to the brim. I took a deep drink, trying to wash away the bullshit I'd just had to deal with.

She was quiet for a long time. "I had to make sure you were okay..."

"I'm fine." I took another drink and turned around, seeing her in my shirt. I crossed my arms over my chest and tilted my chin to the floor, staring at the hardwood floor beneath my feet. "I told you I would call."

"And you didn't." She didn't come close to me, crossing her arms over her chest. "I couldn't go home and go to sleep. I knew I wouldn't be able to stop thinking about you until it was over."

My hands gripped the counter on either side of me, the drink sitting in front of me.

She slowly came closer to me, approaching me with hesitation.

I didn't know why I was being such a dick to her. I was still high on adrenaline, a little drunk from all the booze, and just pissed off about the whole thing. I was angry at myself for not figuring it out on my own, and I was pissed off that Vox was too powerful for me to kill. I punished him in a humiliating way, and if he stepped out of line again, I could kill him—with no resistance.

She moved a little closer, her eyes on my face.

I wouldn't look at her.

Then she spoke, her voice a whisper, and she tore down all my walls. "Babe..."

I closed my eyes when I heard that nickname, the possessive title that made me feel like the luckiest bastard in the entire fucking world. I released the air I'd been holding in my lungs and lifted my gaze to meet hers.

She moved closer, her hands moving to my arms, so she could feel me, squeeze me through my clothes to make sure I wasn't hurt. Her hands glided to my chest then stroked down, making sure everything was exactly as she remembered. The concern in her gaze was undeniable, so sincere that she looked even more beautiful than ever before. She was relieved, but there was still pain in her eyes, like her worst fears were still fresh in her mind.

My problem with Vox was finished, so there was no reason to think about it anymore. I walked in the door and had the most exceptional woman waiting for me, worrying about me. What other man could say something like that? "Baby, I'm okay."

When she knew my anger was gone, she stepped closer, her arms wrapping around my neck. Her forehead nestled into my neck and she hugged me, held me close, her fingers pressing into my warm skin so she could feel my pulse. She rested her face in my chest, breathing deep and steady like she'd just found the peace she'd been looking for.

My arms circled her waist, and I rested my chin on her forehead, enjoying our silent companionship, the deep affection that wrapped around us both. My hand cupped the back of her head, and I pressed a kiss to her forehead, closing my eyes as I felt this tiny woman in my arms.

Peace descended over my soul, a silence I'd never encoun-
tered before. She drove me crazy, turned me into a man I
didn't recognize, but she also gave me this...whatever it
was. My arms tightened around her, and I pulled her
closer, my arm squeezing her harder because I never
wanted to let her go.

Never.

THE TRUCK PULLED up to the entrance.

Steel unbuckled his safety belt.

I grabbed his arm and steadied him. "I'm going alone this
time."

He stilled, his eyes narrowing. "You're gonna carry all that
cash by yourself?"

I dropped my hand and looked out the front windshield.
"I'll call if I need you." I opened the sliding door and
hopped out. When I reached the sidewalk, I turned around
to look at the adjacent roof, to see if the snipers were still
there—even though I knew Damien wouldn't pull that shit
again.

It'd been over a month since the last time I was there. I'd
dreaded it every moment of every day, but now I had to face
it. With my gun in the back of my jeans, I entered the ware-
house, taking the stairs until I descended to the bottom
floor.

His cooks were making the meth in the rear, while his other
workers bagged and prepared to ship everything. They

looked at me, watched me, but they didn't do a damn thing about it.

I entered Damien's office, finding more than just two bags of money.

Now there were twenty.

Damien was behind his desk, the bruise on his head absent because it had healed. One hand rested on the desk, and he tapped his fingers against the surface, as if he was bored waiting for me to show up and make good on my word.

I looked at the bags, kicked a few to make sure they were full.

Damien's hostility had increased since our last visit, and that was obvious without him speaking a single word. His look was more than enough.

I dropped into the chair facing his desk.

He sighed quietly, frustrated I didn't just take the money and leave, frustrated that he would have to hear me speak. He couldn't contain his rage, his green eyes like poisonous venom that he wanted to launch at me.

My knees were wide apart, and I propped one elbow on the armrest, my closed fist resting against the side of my face. I stared at him, feeling his rage rise in the room like smoke to the ceiling.

He finally addressed me. "Aren't your men going to check the bags?"

"Yes. But we're going to talk first."

His eyebrows furrowed. "You won, Heath. Just take your shit and go."

My feelings for Catalina made me look at him differently, especially since he had the exact same eyes she did. I remembered the soft way he spoke to her, the way he offered to take care of her even though she wasn't his responsibility. All my hatred for him died in that moment... and the only person I hated was myself. "This is the last time I'm collecting payment from you."

He took a deep breath, like he assumed that was some kind of threat. "You're going to kill me. You expect me to beg for my life?"

"No. I just don't want to do business with someone like you."

He was still, not breathing.

"Vox has been punished—in the most humiliating way possible." I still preferred to kill him, but that opportunity may come later.

"And now it's my turn," he said with a bored voice. "Shut up and get it over with."

He still didn't get it. "I'm not going to kill you, Damien."

His eyes narrowed.

"I'm dissolving this business relationship."

"Business relationship?" he asked. "Robbing someone doesn't constitute a business relationship."

I ignored the jab. "I'm not coming here anymore, Damien. I won't collect payment. I won't see your fucking face. This is over—simple as that." I pulled my phone out of my pocket so I could call Steel.

Damien was quiet, staring at me for a while as if he didn't understand what I said. "After all of this, all the shit we've been through, you're just gonna stop?" He cocked his head slightly. "What the fuck, Heath?"

"I don't want to be in business with someone who plots against me like that," I said calmly. "Who uses my own man against me. With the termination of this relationship, you will no longer get services from me, and as time goes on, I think you'll understand exactly what I'm talking about." With no representation, competitors would move in— knowing I would do nothing to stop them. Damien would be completely on his own. Hopefully, he could handle it.

Damien stared at me for a long time, reading between the lines. "What the fuck am I missing here?"

I held his gaze.

"You collect millions from me every time you come by. You're just gonna walk away?"

"It's never been about money, Damien." I rose out of the chair.

He shook his head slightly. "So, I never have to see your face again?"

Time would tell. "Probably not."

He leaned back against the chair, more disgruntled by this twist instead of the idea of me killing him. "You're tricking me."

"No."

"Just a month ago, you said you were going to collect all my profits for the next three months...and now you don't want a damn thing from me?"

Damien was smarter than I gave him credit for. Anyone else would just accept the terms because they were happy to keep their cash, but Damien had a suspicious mind. I pulled out my phone and called Steel. "Ready for you." I hung up.

Damien rose from his chair. "I asked you a question."

I unzipped all of the bags. "And I already gave you an answer. It's not my fault you're too stupid to understand what I'm saying."

With his hands against the desk, he stared at me, like he knew something was wrong but couldn't put his finger on it. He searched for an explanation but couldn't find one, couldn't figure out this puzzle.

"You think I'm giving you a break. But once I'm out of the picture, the other guys will move in...and you'll wish you still had me." It wasn't a concrete threat. That might happen, that might not happen, but it was the only legitimate explanation I could give. I left it vague on purpose, so he would take it seriously. "You'll miss me, Damien. You'll see soon enough."

TEN

CATALINA

I OPENED THE FRIDGE AND STARED AT THE CONTENTS, unsure what to make for dinner. I hadn't spoken to Heath all day, but I suspected he would walk in the door at some point, coming into my apartment without needing an invitation.

So, I should probably cook for two.

I wasn't a talented cook like he was, only able to prepare a few simple things, like salads, sandwiches, mac and cheese, stuff like that. Maybe if I continued to wait, he'd come over and cook himself, fixing my problem altogether.

Like he could read my thoughts, the locks turned in the door, and he stepped inside. "Whatcha doing, baby?" One hand was behind his back as he stepped inside.

"Trying to decide what to make for dinner." I shut the fridge door then turned to him. "But now that you're here, I don't need to worry about it." I walked up to him, seeing those blue eyes that looked into mine in all my dreams. My hands planted on his chest, and I rose on my tiptoes to kiss him.

He grinned against my lips. "So, you need me for sex *and* food."

I had no shame. "Yep." I pulled away and noticed that his hand was still behind his back. "What are you hiding?"

"Something for you."

"Ooh...a surprise." I rubbed my palms together. "I wonder what it is."

He pulled his hand forward, revealing an arrangement of sunflowers.

I stared at the yellow petals and the deep black color at the center, taking a few seconds to understand what I was looking at. It was almost the end of October, and these kinds of flowers had disappeared a long time ago.

His confidence started to wane, which was a first. "You don't like them."

"No," I said quickly. "I just don't understand... Where did you find them?" The weather had been dreary and cold, forcing me to ditch my dresses and wear jeans and sweaters, which was so depressing.

"It's a secret."

I took the flowers from his hand and brought them to my nose to smell them. They smelled so good, fresh, like it was still summer.

He watched me smell the petals, his blue eyes transfixed on mine. "You're my sunflower..."

I opened my eyes and looked at him, my fingers holding the long stems.

"You're my summer—all year-round."

I lowered the flowers because I couldn't believe what he'd just said. It was the most romantic thing I'd ever heard, from any movie, book, or anything I saw on social media. And the fact that this rock-hard, cold man said it made it even more romantic. "They're beautiful...I love them." I rose on my tiptoes again and kissed him, feeling my heart ache at the gesture. I turned around and grabbed a vase so I could display them on my counter, adding water so they would live a long time. "Thank you."

He stood on the other side of the kitchen island, staring at me with those blue eyes that reminded me of the summer sky. He watched me shift the flowers in the vase, arranging them perfectly.

"Why is it a secret?"

He shrugged.

"Heath."

He continued to stare at me with the same intensity, but he dropped his gaze for a moment, as if he was preparing to give his answer. "Remember when I told you I have other residences?"

"Yes."

"I have a home in the countryside, twenty acres of land."

I had no idea where this was going. He couldn't grow them in the countryside because it wasn't sunny and warm anywhere.

"I built a greenhouse...so I can grow them all year-round for you." He didn't look me in the eye as he made his confession, like he was embarrassed to say that out loud, even more irritated to hear himself say it.

I suddenly couldn't feel my fingers. Couldn't feel my own heartbeat. I watched him stare at the counter to avoid my gaze, watched him deal with the sudden intensity that had entered the room. Now I couldn't look at him the same, couldn't see him as the sexy piece of man that occupied my bed. He was so much more now...I knew he'd always been more. I just didn't realize.

I moved around the counter and stepped up to him, my hands gripping the sides of his face to force his look on me, to look at me with those blue eyes that were oxygen to my lungs. I pressed my forehead to his chin and closed my eyes, my heart suddenly aching like I was in pain. When I opened my eyes again, I kissed him, kissed him slow and soft.

His arms secured around my waist, and he pulled me close, his large hands digging into me to keep me against his beating heart. He kissed me back, turning into the confident and powerful man I knew. His hands were all over me, his kiss was authoritative.

I jumped up, knowing he would catch me without even looking at me, his mind and body so in sync with mine. His strong arms caught me, and he lifted me onto the island counter, my legs circling his waist.

My hands yanked his shirt over his head, our movements speeding up now that we grew more impatient, more desperate. My nails clawed at his bare back, and I pulled him in to kiss me, my ankles digging into his ass through his jeans.

His lips moved to my neck, and he kissed me as I undid his jeans, his hot breaths in my ear.

I fell into him as he fell into me, getting lost in the storm that surrounded us both. Our dinner was forgotten because neither one of us needed food for sustenance. The only thing we needed was each other—all of each other.

HIS HEAVY BODY was on top of mine, his groan fading away as he finished his orgasm, filling me with his come. His hips flexed slightly, moving his wet dick inside me. His face was close to mine, and he closed his eyes as he recuperated from the pleasure he'd just felt.

My nails were deep in his back, and my crossed ankles were deep against his ass. I kept him close to me because I never wanted him to leave, to pull himself out of me and break this unbelievable connection.

He opened his eyes and looked at me, giving me that intense expression like he wanted to claim me again, even though he already had so many times.

Then my phone started to ring on the nightstand, the noise piercing our silence.

He stared at me.

I didn't reach for the phone, tuned out the sound of it altogether.

"Are you going to get that?" he whispered.

"No." My hands slid up his back and into his hair. "I couldn't care less who's calling me." This man was the only thing that mattered right now. Nobody ever called me, so it was probably spam. But even if it wasn't, I didn't care.

He started to pull out of me.

My ankles tightened, and I secured him against my body. "No..."

His dick had softened inside me, sheathed in his come as well as mine. He brought his face close to mine again, looking into my gaze.

"I like it when you're inside me." I raised my head and kissed his soft lips above mine.

He kissed me back, his hands grabbing mine and pinning them above my head.

Good. I didn't want to go anywhere.

He held himself on top of me, looking into my face. "We've been at this for hours... I need some time." His dick was always hard for me, but after several sessions and many climaxes, he was done for a while.

"I know. I still like you inside me."

His eyes turned affectionate.

"I'm hungry..."

He smiled slightly. "I can make something."

"No." I squeezed his waist.

"Alright, then I guess we'll starve."

"Let's order a pizza or something."

"I really don't mind cooking."

"I know, but that means you'll have to leave…"

He continued to look down at me, his hands around my wrists. "I'll have to leave to answer the door when the pizza arrives."

"Yeah, but that's not for at least thirty minutes."

That slight smile was still on his lips, finding my clinginess endearing rather than annoying. "Alright, let's order a pizza."

I pulled out of his grasp and grabbed my phone. There was an app on my phone, so I opened it and quickly ordered something before I tossed it aside.

His eyes hadn't left mine. "Now what?"

"We just stay like this."

He leaned down and kissed me on the mouth, rubbing his nose against mine. Then he pulled out of me and rolled over, moving to his back beside me.

I turned to him, snuggling into his side.

He rolled in my direction and hiked my thigh over his hips. We were still close together, lying in my dark apartment because there was nothing else we'd rather be doing. I could do this every moment for the rest of my life, just live in this beautiful bubble.

"What did you order?"

"Margherita."

"Sounds good."

My hand moved up his chest until it cupped his cheek, feeling the stubble on his chin. My fingers rubbed across it, feeling the resistance of the thick hair. My fingers touched his lip, stroked his jawline, memorized every detail of his face. "That was really sweet of you..." It was probably the sweetest thing he'd ever done in his entire life.

His eyes didn't react, but he knew exactly what I referred to.

"This winter won't be so bad."

"You'll never be cold, I can tell you that." He turned his lips into my hand, kissing the center of my palm.

My hand slipped down to his chest, and I looked into his eyes, so comfortable that I could fall asleep without having dinner at all. My heartbeat was slow, slower than it was when I slept, and I felt like the sunshine was hitting me right in the face, blanketing me with warm light. There were butterflies in the room, a pleasant breeze from the summer season, a glare from the horizon. I was in a different place, lying in a meadow with this man beside me, watching me, holding me.

"What are you thinking about?" His deep voice came out as a whisper, as if it were an apparition in a dream.

"It's stupid..."

"Nothing you think is stupid."

My hand moved over his chest as I smiled. "For a second, I thought I was in a meadow...in the sunshine...with butterflies and tall blades of grass. Maybe I fell asleep for a second and fell into a dream."

His fingers glided up my stomach, his hand outstretched so it covered me entirely. "Your eyes have been open the whole time, baby."

"Then it wasn't a dream...it was real."

AFTER HE SHOWERED and got ready for the day, he headed to the door. "I have to go, baby."

The flowers were in the vase on the kitchen island, bright yellow and still blooming, filled with the memory of summer. When the sun was out, those flowers helped me believe it wasn't sixty degrees outside, but swelteringly hot instead. "No." I moved in front of the door, blocking it with my body.

He tried not to laugh at my pathetic attempt to keep him here. "You know I would stay if I could."

I moved into his chest and wrapped my arms around his neck. "Please..."

He sighed deeply, like he might abandon everything just to stay with me. "Don't make this hard for me."

"No, I'm going to." I kissed him good on the mouth, giving him openmouthed kisses that would entice him to come back to bed with me.

He almost fell for it, but he pulled his lips away and saw reason. "Nice try. You almost got me." He cupped my cheeks and kissed my forehead before he moved to the door. "I've got a lot to do today. Come over later tonight."

"When will you be home?"

He shrugged. "Sometime after seven."

"Alright." Sometimes I wished he lived with me. That way, I would see him every single day; I would never have to go long until he walked through the door again.

His hand moved into my hair, and he placed his forehead against mine. He kept it there for a long time, closing his eyes as he held me in my entryway. Then he kissed me goodbye, a gentle kiss that didn't linger and turn into more.

"Bye." I watched him walk out and shut the door behind himself.

I stood there, devastated, as if he'd just walked out of my life for good.

PATRICIA LET ME INSIDE. "Hey, Catalina. I'll let your father know you're here."

"Actually, I'm just here to see my brother. Has he come home yet?"

"About thirty minutes ago." She stood in jeans and a nice blouse, looking nothing like a housekeeper when she wore cute clothes like that.

"Anna?"

"She hasn't come home yet." She examined my face, knowing something was wrong. "Everything alright, honey?"

"Yeah, just a long day." I turned to the stairs. "I'll let myself up."

"Alright. Your father is taking a nap anyway. He'll probably be awake by the time you're finished."

I took the stairs to the third floor. There was a maroon rug down the long hallway, over the dark hardwood floor. The right side was all windows and paintings in between, and the guest bedrooms were on another floor.

I approached the door but didn't knock.

I almost turned around and left.

But I stood there, determined to do this, determined to have this conversation. I knocked.

"Yeah?" His response was immediate.

I opened the door and poked my head inside.

He sat at the dining table with his laptop in front of him, shirtless because he never seemed to wear clothes when he was home. It reminded me of Heath, who was hardly ever dressed when we stayed in together. "Is this a bad time?"

He shut his laptop. "Why don't you ever call before you stop by?"

"You never tell me you're coming to my performances. You just show up."

"That's a public event—not my private home." He got out of the chair and walked inside his closet.

I took that as an invitation and sank into the chair across from his.

When he returned, his naked chest was covered by a gray shirt. His eyes didn't give me any warmth before he sat across from me. Last time we saw each other, he offered to let me move in, to buy me my own place, but now he was back to business as usual. "I think Dad's taking a nap."

"Yeah, that's what Patricia told me."

He pushed the laptop aside and looked out the window for a second. "Nice to see you in jeans and a sweater." He turned back to me.

"Yeah. I'm comfortable."

He cocked his head slightly to the side, looking into my face as if he saw something he needed to hang on to. "Something wrong, Cat?"

Now that I was face-to-face with him, looking into my mother's eyes, seeing so much of myself in him, I was more nervous than before. There was time to turn back, to abandon this idea, but I continued to sit there. "Actually, there's something I wanted to talk to you about..."

He cocked his head again, his eyes even more focused than they were before.

"I need you to do me a favor."

"Anything," he said immediately. "Whatever you want."

That was a good answer. "Alright... I need you to stay calm. I need you to listen to everything I have to say, to remember that I'm your sister, that I wouldn't come to you with this unless it was important to me."

His eyes narrowed slightly. "Jesus…" He looked away for a moment, sighing loudly as he prepared for whatever bomb I was about to drop on his shoulders. His fingers pinched the bridge of his nose before he dragged his fingers to his lips.

"Damien."

"Please don't tell me you're pregnant…"

I shot him a glare. "Damien, I'm being serious."

"So, you aren't pregnant?" he asked.

"No," I snapped.

He released a sigh, like that was the thing he was most afraid of.

"Promise me."

"You're scaring me, sis."

"Well…it's not good news."

He looked away again, taking a deep breath before he turned to me. After a few seconds, he was still, collected, ready. "Please tell me you aren't sick—"

"Nothing like that."

He relaxed further, his hands coming together in his lap as he regarded me. He gave me a slight nod, an invitation to speak.

Now, I had the floor.

Fuck, I had the floor. "Alright…I don't know where to start."

He stayed quiet, doing as I asked by staying calm and patient. His green eyes were glued to mine, still like a living statue.

"Well, I'm seeing someone."

All he did was take a breath.

"And I really like him. We've been seeing each other for a while...and he makes me happy."

Damien kept the same expression. "But I'm not going to like him, am I?"

I shook my head. "No..."

He curled his bottom lip into his mouth as he made a strained expression, like he was doing everything he could to follow my directions. "Who is he?"

I didn't want to say. I knew Damien wouldn't be able to keep his word once the name was in the air. "Heath..."

Damien had no reaction whatsoever—as if he were in shock.

"I know you have your differences. I know you have your reasons to dislike him. But as your sister...I'm asking you to let that go. This is the man I want to be with. I know you love me, and I love you...and I need you to do this for me. Please."

Damien still didn't react. Didn't even take a breath. His eyes hadn't blinked once, and he continued to stare at me, his green eyes like two probes looking into mine.

"I know he's done terrible things. But he didn't directly take Anna. He didn't directly break in to your house. He was an accomplice to all that, and now that all of that is in the past...I'd like it if you could let it go. And the money you pay him... It's just money." As I heard myself speak, I realized how much I was asking of him, to release a year of vendettas.

He straightened in the chair, his hands moving to the surface of the table. His elbows planted, and his fingers interlocked in front of his lips, his eyes still on me, still not blinking. He stared for a long time, his hostility low but potent. He lowered his hands. "Last week, he came to collect his payment...and told me it was the last time he would do so." He shook his head slightly. "I knew it was odd. I knew I was missing something. And now it all makes sense." His fingers returned to his lips, and he stared at me again, the cogs in his brain working. "And the last time he came, everything went according to plan...until something changed. My snipers were ready to take him out, but on the camera feed, it showed he got a phone call...that was *you* who called. You eavesdropped on my conversation and told him everything."

I refused to lie about it, but I didn't confess to it either. I'd suspected he would piece everything together after I came clean, so I wasn't surprised he came to that conclusion so quickly. He was a smart man.

"That was why he didn't kill me."

I had no idea that Heath had let my brother off the hook, that he stopped collecting payment. There was only one reason why he would do that. I just didn't understand why Heath didn't tell me. "If he's stopped collecting payment from you and the past is in the past, I'd like it if you could let this go. I know it's a lot to ask, Damien. But I wouldn't be asking you to do this for me unless it was important to me." I had to put faith in my brother's love for me, to hope that love was stronger than his hate.

He leaned back in the chair, his gaze moving out the window while the same stoic expression was burned into his face. His green eyes reflected the sunlight, and the tightness of his jaw indicated the way he ground his teeth together.

"Damien...please."

He eventually turned back to me, taking a deep breath. "No."

I closed my eyes and felt utterly defeated.

"I can let go of most of the shit he's done—but not all. But I despise a man who's not honest about who he is, who doesn't come clean to the woman he's sleeping with about the shit he's really done. I know you don't know everything, because if you did, you wouldn't be sitting here right now. You'd want nothing to do with him."

Adrenaline dumped into my blood, and my chest started to rise higher, to suck in all the oxygen that my brain suddenly needed. I thought I was the one catching Damien off guard, but it was the other way around.

And I was scared.

His eyes narrowed, like he was disappointed in me. "He lied to you. He tricked you. Now, you're sitting in front of me, fighting for a man you don't even know. It's fucking humiliating. I'm humiliated for you."

My breathing continued to speed up. "What did he do?"

His furious eyes burned into mine. "When I refused to pay him, he took someone very special to me, took someone to execute. You know who that was?"

Hades? Anna?

"Dad."

My heart fell.

"He took him to another location and intended to shoot him in the back of the head—to punish me. You want to know the only reason that didn't happen?"

Oh my god.

"It was because Hades got there first. Hades got there, killed the guard, and saved Dad's life." He leaned forward. "Dad would be dead right now if I didn't make the right calls. Heath would have executed an innocent old man." He fell back into the chair. "If you wanted to be with someone like me, I wouldn't give a damn. Not all criminals are evil. I don't hurt innocent people, and I don't kill cops. I stay in my world and never cross that line." His hand straightened and fell onto the table, mimicking a line with his straight fingers. "But that motherfucker crossed the line. He doesn't stay in his lane. He tried to murder a harmless, sweet man—*for money*. No, I'll never let that go. I'll never forget that he nearly killed my father. I'll never forgive, never forget. And now that you know the truth, you'll see what he really is— and dump his ass." His eyes shifted back and forth as he looked in mine. "He played you like a fool, Catalina."

I did my best not to cry, but the truth was so overwhelming. The idea of someone doing that to my father, my best friend, made me so sick that I couldn't keep my lunch down. And the fact that it was Heath who did it, who fucked me without telling me the truth, who omitted that critical piece of information from me...made me feel as stupid as Damien had predicted I would.

"You betrayed your own brother—for him." His hand rested on the table, tightening into a fist. "You betrayed your own family. That's not you, but he got into your head and turned you into a disloyal, stupid girl."

Tears splashed down my cheeks.

But my brother gave me no pity. "I'm gonna kill him for what he did to *our* father. I don't care if he stops collecting my cash. I don't care if he apologizes. I don't care if he steps down as the Skull King and gives me every coin to his name. He. Crossed. The. Line." He slammed his fist onto the table, bringing his speech to a close.

I held my breath so I would stop crying, but that only halted it for a few seconds. My chest started to rock, like water slamming into the doors of a dam. The doors flung open and my tears spilled out, turning into soul-crushing sobs. I covered my face because I couldn't stand the way my brother looked at me, as if he'd never been so disappointed in me, as if he didn't even know me anymore, as if he'd lost all respect for me.

I couldn't stop crying.

I couldn't stop the pain.

When I pulled my hands away from my face, I saw Damien looking out the window, indifferent to my tears. He didn't want to touch me, didn't want to comfort me. He was disgusted by my betrayal.

I'd chosen Heath over my brother, and it'd all been for nothing,

Heath lied to me...and destroyed me.

ELEVEN

HEATH

I PARKED THE TRUCK IN THE GARAGE AND NOTICED HER car wasn't there. I was two hours later than I said I would be, so I hoped she didn't grow impatient and leave. There was a well-stocked fridge and pantry, along with a huge tub for her to take a bubble bath, so she had lots of reasons to stay—even if I weren't there.

I was disappointed.

I'd been looking forward to this moment all day, as if I hadn't slept over last night, as if I hadn't been with her just eight hours ago.

I took the stairs to the next level.

When I rose to the top, I saw her.

She stood on the other side of my kitchen island, her arms across her chest, her eyes furious.

The energy in the room was different, so unusual I couldn't even describe it. It was sunny outside but a hailstorm on the inside. She was still, but her energy twisted around like a tornado. And the way she looked at me...with blinding fury.

I halted as I stared at her, immediately detecting every hint of her rage.

She started to breathe hard, her chest rising and falling as she sucked in more air to prepare her for whatever her intentions were. Her eyes were wide open and coated in moisture, but not from tears, just emotional rage.

I stepped farther inside. "Baby—"

"Don't ever call me that again." The words tumbled out of her mouth like a somersault, quickly unfurling without taking a breath. There was a wooden block of knives in front of her, like she wanted to stay close so she could grab a blade if she needed it.

This wasn't the kind of reaction she'd given in the past when she lost her mind to hysterical jealousy. She wouldn't stand that far away from me. She wouldn't wait in my house until I got home to speak her mind. She would ignore me until I came after her.

That meant something else had happened.

It took me only a few seconds to figure it out. She knew.

She fucking knew.

I stepped closer to her, my eyes locked on hers. "Catalina—"

"Damien told me everything!" she shouted, her yells making the walls vibrate the way mine did. "How fucking *dare* you? How fucking dare you touch my father? What the hell is wrong with you?"

When I'd pulled into the garage just minutes ago, my life was different. I was happy, coming home to the woman who took full occupation of my life. But now it felt like an eternity had passed...like it was a whole different lifetime. Even though I was about to lose everything, I stayed calm. "That was a long time ago—"

"And that makes it okay?" she hissed. "You lied to me, Heath. You fucked me and lied to me. You used me. You humiliated me." Tears started to streak down my cheeks. "Do you have any idea how fucking stupid I looked, asking my brother to put aside your differences so I could be with you? Then he told me *that*...and I sat there like a fucking dumbass."

"You weren't supposed to tell him—"

"So you could keep screwing me?" The tears made streams down her cheeks and dripped to her chin, ruining her makeup along the way. "Was this another part of your vengeance? To screw his sister to stick it to him?"

That was fucking offensive. "No. But if you were really going to talk to him about it, I would have come clean and explained why you couldn't do that. You didn't talk to me. You didn't include me in the discussion."

"He's my brother. I don't have to include you in the discussion."

"But I'm in this relationship with you."

"Relationship?" Now, her voice turned quiet, like I'd said something that stabbed her in the gut. "This was never a relationship. How could you give it that description when you didn't tell me what you did? And you were obviously never going to."

I didn't lie about it. "No...I wasn't going to."

Her eyes widened like she couldn't believe I'd actually said it. "Wow...you're evil." Her palms moved to her face, and she gave a hysterical laugh packed with emotion before she dropped her hands, fresh tears on her face. "God, I'm so fucking stupid..."

"This is why I wasn't going to tell you. Because I knew you would never get past it."

"Damn right!" She threw her arms down. "How can you sleep at night? How can you be with a woman and look her in the eye every night while knowing she would never even touch you if she knew the truth?" It was a rhetorical question, cutting deep.

"Because neither one of us expected it to turn into this, Catalina." I came closer to her so we wouldn't have to scream at each other from opposite sides of the kitchen. "I thought we would last a few weeks then forget about each other. I thought we would mean nothing to each other, that you would be another notch on my bedpost, as I would be on yours. And the longer it went on, the more difficult it became to confess. Because every time I thought about it, I knew what your reaction would be, that you would never forgive me. So, I didn't tell you...in order to keep you as long as possible."

She shook her head, her expression filled with disgust.

"For the first time in my life, I'm happy...and I didn't want to lose that." I put all my cards on the table, aimed for the stars even though there was no chance I could fix this.

"And you chose your own happiness over mine. Now, I have to live with this, to watch Damien look at me with disgust, to be with my father and know what my lover had intended to do to him. I have to live with this." She slammed both of her palms against her chest. "You lied to me. You tricked me—"

"And you were just as happy as I was, Catalina."

Her eyes narrowed and she stepped back. "You're an asshole, Heath. I don't mean that playfully anymore. I mean that literally. You were the man I trusted most in the world, and you betrayed me. After all that bullshit about needing to trust you...you were lying to my face." She shook her head again. "I hate you. I fucking hate you." Tears welled up in the corners of her eyes before they fell.

That hurt...really fucking bad. "No, you don't."

"Oh, trust me, I do."

"Catalina—"

"I betrayed my own brother for you. I made that phone call when I should have kept my mouth shut. And if I'd known all the facts, I would have let him kill you. I regret that now...will have to live with that regret for the rest of my life."

I took a deep breath as her words hit me like a thousand blades. "I would take it back if I could, alright? And that's not who I am anymore. Let's not forget I released you from that cage when I didn't have to. The night we met, I changed. I didn't even know you, and I changed for you. I rescued you from that basement and freed all those women—"

"Because I told you to."

"But then I banned the practice throughout the entire country." I slammed my hand into my chest. "Because I wanted to. Because just the idea of that shit happening makes me sick to my stomach. Look, I'm different now. Don't hate me for something I did before I even knew you. Catalina, come on—"

"Fuck you, Heath."

"I know I should have told you the truth, but if I had, I would have lost you—"

"Then what was your brilliant plan?" she snapped. "To never tell me, to keep making excuses? For how long?"

"Years...if I could manage it."

She shook her head again.

"You told me you didn't want a husband until you were thirty, so I didn't see the harm in wasting your time."

She stared at me with disgust. "Didn't see the *harm*?"

"I know it's terrible. I know it's wrong. I know how fucking terrible it sounds as I say it out loud. But I fell in love with you...and I wanted to do everything possible to keep you, to hold on to that as long as I could."

Her breathing stopped altogether, even her tears halted on her cheeks, as if gravity lost all its force. "What?"

I shook my head. "Don't play that game."

"Game?"

"Don't act like you didn't know I was madly in love with you. You're too fucking smart for that. You know we stopped fucking a long time ago, that we've been making love ever since. You think I'm growing flowers for you because I think you have a nice ass?" I asked incredulously. "You think I get jealous of that short-shit director because you're just some woman I'm sleeping with? You think you're the only person who has the key and code to my private home because you get my dick wet? Come on, Catalina. Knock that shit off."

She breathed hard, her arms crossing over her chest. "You promised me..."

I had to stop myself from rolling my eyes. "Well, you fell in love with me first."

"What are you talking about?"

"When you called me and warned me about Damien. That was the moment I knew."

She shut her mouth tightly, and this time, she averted her gaze, like she couldn't confront reality. It was too traumatic. "You promised me, Heath."

"Don't expect me to feel bad about it. Because I don't." I stared at her twelve feet away from me, devastatingly beautiful with those tears making her eyes wet and her cheeks red. Women never looked attractive like that, but she was irresistible.

She put her fingers under her eyes and wiped up her makeup, even though that wouldn't make much of a difference because the damage had been done.

"I will do anything to make this work. I'll apologize to Damien. I'll apologize to your father. Anything you want."

She turned back to me, her eyes cold. "You think an apology is going to fix everything? You literally tried to kill my father. He would be dead right now if Damien hadn't protected him. I would have no parents right now—because of you." She pointed her finger at me. "And you think an apology is going to make that go away?"

I already knew I'd lost her—and it fucking hurt.

"In case you haven't noticed, my father is my best fucking friend."

"Yeah...I noticed." Another reason I'd kept my mouth shut.

"So, no, Heath. An apology doesn't change anything. I will never look at you the same..."

"Love is much stronger than hate, Catalina." I stepped closer to her.

She shook her head, her eyes furious. "It was never love, Heath. You can't fall in love with someone you don't know."

"You do know me." My hand moved over my chest. "Everything between us, it was all real."

"I hate you," she snapped. "I hate you..." She continued to say the phrase, backing away from me, staring at me like she meant it. "I thought I was crazy, told myself it was a stupid superstitious belief, but it was the truth. I should have taken it seriously. I should have listened...and that's my biggest regret."

I vaguely remembered her mentioning this when we first got together, when she made me promise not to fall in love with her. She never elaborated and never mentioned it again. "Take what seriously?"

She backed up farther, staring at me with ferocity. "Hades and Damien went to Marrakech a long time ago. A gypsy read their fortune, said they would fall in love, but it would be painful. Neither one of them believed it, until everything she said came true. So, I visited the same gypsy with Damien a while ago, when he asked her for help with Anna. She told me my fortune."

Did she really believe that bullshit?

"She said I would only fall in love once, and he would be an enemy to my family." She looked into my eyes as if she identified me as that man. "That was why I told you not to fall in love with me, because I was afraid it was true. And it was. That's why I've never tried to fall in love, never stayed with a man long enough for it to happen because I knew it wasn't possible. And when I did find a man to marry, it would be based on friendship, trust, and compatibility. Now...I know it's true. That's why I turned you down so many times, until you wore me down. The prophecy was true..."

"Catalina, don't let some stranger dictate your life. You're smarter than that—"

"It happened to both Damien and Hades. You think that's a coincidence?"

"Yes."

"And the fact that everything she said about me is true?"

I considered my answer for a long time. "What does it matter if it's true? If she says I'm the only man you're going to love, then you should try to make this work with me. You should fight for me."

She stepped away, moving to a different side of the kitchen island. "No. She said it would never work—and it won't work."

I didn't want to lose her. I couldn't picture my life without her. I couldn't imagine going back to the whores I used to pay to bed me. I didn't want to go back to that numb existence. I couldn't do it. "Please." I'd never begged for anything in my life.

"I despise you." She said it without skipping a beat. "I don't trust you. I don't respect you. And I'll always hate you for what you did to my innocent father."

"He's still alive—"

"Because of Damien. Not you." She kept the knives in front of her, as if she would actually draw one on me. "I hate you."

"You don't hate me. You love me."

She refused to acknowledge those feelings ever existed. "No." She stared at me with a hard expression, ice-cold. "You mean nothing to me, Heath. I know where my allegiance lies...and it's not with you."

I kept the same expression, but I was falling apart inside, knowing this woman was already gone even though she was still in my home. That all I had of her was a memory, not the real thing.

"I don't care about the way you make money. Damien and Hades aren't upstanding citizens. But they don't hurt innocent people like you. You're my enemy as far as I'm concerned. What we had…it's in the past. It's like it never happened at all. Because I see you for what you really are. I just wish you were man enough to be honest with me, so I didn't have to learn this lesson the hard way."

"Baby—"

"Call me that again, and I'll stab you." She spoke calmly, like it was a matter of fact rather than an emotional outburst.

My breathing started to speed up because I knew she was about to walk away from me forever—and there was nothing I could do to make her stay.

"Don't come to my apartment. Don't fucking use your key to come and go as you please. Don't call me. Don't text me. Don't show up at my performances and confront me backstage, because I will make a scene. You're my enemy now, and I won't make the mistakes I made before. I won't stop Damien from killing you. I'll even help him if I can. So, it's in your best interest to disappear from my life." She turned her back to me and headed for the stairs.

I was paralyzed on the spot, my chest caving in with agony. I'd never felt pain like this, not from a stab wound, not from a bullet, not from any physical injury in my life. It was indescribable…like my entire purpose for being alive was walking away. "Catalina."

She stopped at the top of the stairs and turned to look at me. With one hand on the rail, she held her position, staring at me with icy coldness. The spontaneous and passionate woman I used to know was gone, dead the instant she knew what I did. She didn't look at me the way she used to, like she was so deeply in love that it completely consumed her. Her fire was out, the fire that used to keep me warm.

"I love you." I only got to say it to her a few times, and I'd thought if I ever did, it would happen much differently, with her in my arms and then underneath me, making love all night as she whispered it back to me. But I'd never gotten to hear the words echo back at me...and now I never would. "And I always will."

TWELVE

CATALINA

I walked to my trash can with the leftovers from my sandwich and pressed my foot on the pedal at the base so the lid would pop open. Before I dropped the scraps, I saw the sunflowers I'd dumped days ago.

I dropped the sandwich right on top of the last visible petals then walked away. The dish was placed in the sink so I could wash it later. Then I walked to the couch, my hair pulled up in a bun, and I drank my wine as I watched TV.

I felt so numb.

The body had fascinating ways of protecting itself, of turning off everything when life was too traumatic to experience in full. Maybe that was why I didn't feel anything at all, as if nothing had happened. Or maybe Heath's betrayal was so potent that it changed my feelings instantly, made me see that relationship from a different perspective. Because I didn't think about him. I didn't miss him. I didn't question my decision.

I didn't feel anything at all.

At the time, I thought that was the most passionate relationship of my life, the kind of relationship that would make you feel alive when nothing else did. I thought it would be a good memory someday, a source of heat when the rest of my life turned cold. But now it was just a big fucking mistake.

Fuck him.

I felt so stupid for my actions, felt so stupid for ever feeling anything toward him. I'd loved him at one point, but that was under different circumstances. If those circumstances changed, how could I still love him?

I couldn't.

History had been rewritten, and now so had my feelings.

A week had passed since our conclusion, and he'd done as I asked. He didn't try to contact me, didn't show up at my apartment, didn't do any of that obnoxious stuff...thank god. If he showed his face, I might actually shoot him.

I did have a gun—the one he gave me.

A knock sounded on my door.

I turned at the sound, slightly dreading the person on the other side. I set down my glass of wine and walked to the front door. I looked through the peephole and saw my brother on the other side.

I unlocked all the bolts and opened the door. "Hey." I hadn't seen him since that conversation in his bedroom. I knew it would be awkward the first time we saw each other, so I tried to push past it.

He held up a bottle of wine. "I saw Conway Barsetti today. He gifted this to me, but I thought you would enjoy it more."

I grabbed it by the neck and looked at the year. "Wow, it's like thirty years old."

"The harvest of his birth year. His father bottled a bunch of it and keeps it in his cellar."

"That's sweet."

"Yeah. I knew you'd appreciate it."

"I'm not sure I can open it now." I clutched it to my chest. "I'll have to save it for a special occasion or something."

He shrugged. "Being alive is a special occasion, isn't it?"

I walked to the kitchen and placed it in the pantry. "I'll save it for my wedding or something..." I selected a different bottle, something less fancy, and grabbed two glasses. "You want some?"

"Sure. But next time, I'll get you something you'll actually enjoy." He approached the kitchen and took the glass from me.

"It's very thoughtful, Damien. Thank you." I took a drink, letting the fruity taste of the berries drown my tongue. I licked my lips and looked at the bottle before I looked at him again. "So, what brings you here?"

"Just wanted to see you."

"We both know you never want to see me," I teased.

He drank from his glass and continued to look at me. "How are you?"

"I'm fine," I said quickly.

He stared at me like that answer wasn't good enough.

"I confronted him right after we spoke. It's over." The rest of the details didn't matter. He was gone for good.

"Has he bothered you?"

I shook my head. "I told him not to."

Damien nodded slightly. "Sounds like a clean break."

"I guess." I swirled the wine in my glass.

My brother watched me for a while, being soft rather than cruel. Last time we spoke, he was so angry with me. But the distance over the last week seemed to calm him down. "You're doing better than I expected you to be."

I shrugged. "When you first told me, that was the hardest part. That was the most painful part. But once that passed, everything died inside me. I didn't see him the same anymore, and when I confronted him, that was exactly how I felt. It's like...I stopped feeling everything."

He stared at his glass of wine as he listened.

"He said being with me wasn't a ploy to stick it to you. He just didn't tell me because he knew I would leave him once I knew."

He took a drink, his eyes still down.

"So, that was it."

He raised his head to look at me. "I'm sorry I was so harsh with you. I know that you didn't do any of this on purpose, that he misled you, and that it doesn't mean you're stupid."

My protective brother was back, looking at me like his little sister again. "Don't beat yourself up over it."

I inhaled a deep breath. "It's hard not to..."

"Don't."

"I feel so stupid for calling him. If I hadn't, you would have killed him...and he should be dead right now." Losing my mother when she was so young was already difficult enough. The idea of losing my father in an even more brutal way...disturbed me. Heath almost took away the first man I'd ever loved...and I let him touch me.

"He'll be dead soon enough." He watched my reaction to his words.

But I had no reaction. "Did he hurt Dad?"

"No. When I got there, Dad didn't understand the severity of the situation. You know how he is, thinks everything's a joke. So, I doubt they did anything more than grab him by the arm."

"Why didn't you tell me?"

"I didn't know you were sleeping with him."

"I mean, why didn't you tell me what happened to Dad?"

He looked down into his glass. "Didn't want to scare you."

"Is that the real reason you had him move in with you?"

He nodded.

I closed my eyes as the anger washed over me. Heath had terrorized my family for a long time. "How did this all start?"

"Hades and I were running the business like usual when a psychopath made our lives difficult. His name was Maddox. Balto was the Skull King at the time, but he was at war with someone else that required all his attention, so he didn't defuse the problem with Maddox when he normally would have. Then he stepped down, Heath stepped in, and things were pandemonium for a while. But once the dust settled, Heath expected me to start paying him a cut of my business. I refused because they didn't supply the services they promised when I needed them. It escalated from there..." He grabbed the bottle and refilled his glass. "He continued to threaten me, and I refused to pay. After the third time, he ambushed me at a bar. One of his men had taken Dad to a different location. Heath said he would execute Dad because of my crimes. When I gave in and offered to pay whatever he wanted, he didn't care. He said he was going to kill him anyway..."

I closed my eyes in pain, imagining my father tied up. "How did you get out of that?"

"I'd called Balto right before and asked for help."

"But why would he help you?" Why would he betray his own twin?

"I saved his life once, so I asked him to return the favor." He took a deep drink and licked his lips. "If Balto hadn't honored the request, Dad would be gone. Since Balto was the previous Skull King, he had the right contacts to track Dad's location, but he was too far away, so he called Hades. And Hades took care of it. Balto came to the bar and made Heath stand down."

I couldn't believe the story, couldn't believe the history that Damien had with the man I'd been sleeping with. "I don't know what to say…"

"If I had told you the truth, none of this would have happened. I should have told you…"

"There was no way for you to anticipate any of this."

He continued to drink his wine, his hands resting on the surface of the counter. He was in a long-sleeved shirt with jeans, like he'd gotten off work and went home before he came here. "A part of me doesn't want the answer, but…how did this happen with Heath?"

I'd never told Damien what Heath did to protect him, but now I didn't feel any obligation toward him. "When Anna was gone, Heath kidnapped me. He waited until I left the theater before he grabbed me by my car."

Damien stilled, as if he hadn't expected me to say anything like that.

"He put me in a cage in his basement, we argued a lot, but then he let me go…"

Damien was still speechless.

"His plan was to have you choose between me and Anna. You could surrender, and he would release me…or he'd kill me. Or you could let me die and keep trying to save Anna."

He bowed his head and sighed, anger moving into his eyes.

"But he listened to me pray for your safety and decided to go ahead and release me. He told Liam to fight you in the ring instead. That was how that happened."

Damien stepped back and paced a few steps in front of my kitchen, his hand dragging down his face to his lips.

"We ran into each other weeks later, started talking. He asked me out, and I said no. That kept happening over and over. Then I changed my mind..." I omitted the truth about my captivity by the traffickers because that would be too much for Damien to handle. "It was supposed to be a fling and nothing more, something that was supposed to burn out after a couple of weeks, but it didn't."

Damien came back to me, sighing deeply. "Jesus Christ..."

"I saw a different side to Heath. I saw that he was kind, compassionate, good...so I forgave him for all the things he'd done. The ones I knew about anyway. But when you told me about Dad...I couldn't look past it. It was too terrible."

He raised his head and looked at me. "Did you love him?"

It was such an intimate question that I didn't know how to answer.

"Because you told him about my plan, and I don't see any other reason why you would have done that."

I didn't deny it. "I don't feel that way anymore." I dropped my gaze. "Everything is different now."

He gave a slight nod. "Good."

"Now I don't feel like I ever knew him..." He'd lied to me, every single day. "He said he fell in love with me, and that was the reason he didn't tell me the truth as our relationship continued...because he didn't want to lose me."

Damien didn't blink at that information. "I don't believe that. Not for a second."

I didn't know what I believed. "It doesn't matter anyway."

"I'm going to make him pay for everything he's done to our family, for what he's done to our father, me, you..." He stared at the ground. "I'm going to kill him. And this time, you better not intervene."

"Trust me." I took a drink from my glass. "I won't."

I SAT at the table and enjoyed my drink while the girls talked about the performance we'd finished just a few hours ago. This was my second drink, another I hadn't paid for, and I downed it quickly so I could get that nice buzz.

"I haven't seen you with Heath in a while," Tracy said. "Is he coming tonight?"

"No," I said quickly. "I dumped him." The words came out of my mouth easily, tumbling out like they meant nothing to me at all.

Concern moved into her eyes. "Oh my god, what happened?"

"I broke up with him," I said simply. "It wasn't working."

"Wow...I'm sorry."

"Don't be." I looked into my drink, pouting my lips when I saw it was empty. Now I had to walk my ass to the bar if I wanted another. Or I could wait until someone bought me another. "It was just a fling. I'm over it."

"But he was so hot. Like, insanely hot."

I shrugged. "There're lots of hot guys out there."

"Ugh, not like him," she said. "He was a whole different level."

"Then why don't you go out with him?" He was a manipulative liar, a murderer of innocent people, a complete piece of shit.

"Because..." She looked past me, losing her train of thought. "It looks like you're the only one he wants to talk to."

I stopped licking the last few drops of my drink then gave her a confused expression. When her gaze continued to focus on something past me, I looked over my shoulder.

He sat alone at a nearby table, his vodka beside him. He was in a long-sleeved shirt and jeans, staring at me like he'd been there for a while, looking at my back in the hope I would notice him eventually.

I turned back to her. "That motherfucker..." I got out of my chair and strutted to him, ready to break his nose with my iron fist.

He rose from his chair so he could meet my look head on.

"What the hell did I say?" I snapped, yelling over the music. "I told you not to—"

"Go to your apartment, your performance, or call or text. You didn't say anything about running into you at a bar."

I was not in the mood for his smartass remarks. "I'm not amused."

"Wasn't trying to amuse you." His eyes looked into mine like he hadn't seen me in years. It'd only been weeks, but he stared at my features like he'd never really looked at them before. "You look beautiful."

I made a disgusted face. "Leave me alone, Heath."

"You came over here."

"Fine." I turned around. "Then enjoy your night—"

"Catalina." He grabbed me by the elbow.

I turned at the touch, slamming my closed fist hard into his nose.

His head flew back slightly, but he didn't make a sound, even when his nose started to bleed.

"Don't touch me."

He looked at me as the blood dripped to the top of his lip. He rubbed it away with his sleeve but didn't show a hint of anger at my actions.

"Touch me again, and I'll break your balls."

"I just want to talk to you." When his nose continued to bleed, he wiped away the blood again.

"And say what?" I asked. "I told you I want nothing to do with you."

"I thought you needed a few weeks to cool off."

"Cool off?" I asked. "I'm not angry, Heath. I'm just indifferent to you."

His eyes showed signs of pain, narrowing on my face like my words hurt more than the punch. "That's not me. You know that's not me. The man I am now is the man you've been with for months. That's me."

"If someone murders someone, gets away with it, and then becomes the Pope, does that mean it doesn't matter that he killed someone decades ago?" I asked incredulously.

He sighed loudly. "I didn't murder your father."

"But you're still a sick son of a bitch for trying." I turned around to walk back to the table.

This time, he blocked my path with his size, but he didn't actually touch me. "You know what I've been doing the last few weeks? I've been miserable. Fucking miserable. And I know you have too."

"I've been fine," I said with a straight face. "Absolutely fine."

His nostrils flared. "You're still angry, I get it."

"I'm not angry. I just hate you."

"No, you don't."

"Why is that so hard to believe?" After what he did, it was the most appropriate feeling I should experience.

"It's not that it's *hard* to believe. It's *impossible* to believe."

I rolled my eyes. "Damien told me everything about that night, how the only reason my father is alive right now is because your brother owed him a favor. And I told him you threw me in a cage."

"Did you tell him I let you out?"

"Yes. But again, doesn't excuse what you did in the first place." I tried to move around him.

He positioned himself in front of me. "Please." His pupils contracted as he looked into my eyes. "I'll do anything you want to make this right. I'll step down as the Skull King. I'll make any sacrifice you want me to make—"

"Okay, *Romeo*." I held up my hand to shut him up.

His nostrils flared again.

"I don't want you. It's that simple." I dropped my hand, needing him to understand my stance on the issue perfectly. "I'll never want the man who did that to my own father. I'll never want the man who's harassed my brother. I'll never want the man who didn't have the balls to be honest with me. Do you get it?"

He looked more anguished now than he did when I walked out of his house. His breathing was deep and labored, like he wanted to grab the nearby table and break it in two. "Then, what's your plan? To go back to the losers who don't know how to please a woman? To be with some boring jackass who works in an office somewhere? To be with a plain man? To have a plain life? No, you deserve more than that."

"Maybe I do. And I definitely deserve better than you."

He dropped his gaze for a moment, like I'd hurt him again. "If I'm the only man you'll ever love, there's a reason for that. It's because we're supposed to be together. I don't believe in fate and destiny, all that other bullshit you see in movies, but I believe that. You." He pointed at me then pointed at himself. "Me. We're supposed to be together."

I shook my head. "If that's true, then God must really hate me."

"Don't say that..."

"Please leave me alone, Heath." I gave him a bored look, showing him just how little I cared about this conversation. "I'm over it. You tricked me, played me for a fool, hurt my brother again by hurting me, and I'm done with it. We're all done with it."

"I didn't trick you... I love you."

I rolled my eyes. "No, you don't."

"Yes, I do—"

"A man like you is incapable of love. You never would have touched my father if you weren't completely evil."

Seconds passed as he stared at me. "You're right. I was incapable of love. Until I met you."

"Wow, what a line."

"I'm serious," he snapped. "I swear to fucking god, the moment we met, the moment I laid eyes on you...I was different. I let you go because you were already inside my soul before we even crossed paths. I'm still fighting for you because I believe in that, whatever we had. I understand you're angry and I understand if you need space, but I need you to work with me on this. Please."

"No." I stepped back. "Do I need to spell it out for you? N-O. No."

He bowed his head and rubbed the back of his neck.

"It's not a matter of forgiveness. It's not a matter of letting the past go."

He raised his head and looked at me.

"I don't feel the same way anymore. Whatever I felt for you died when Damien told me the truth. You kidnapped me, put me in a cage, and I let that go. You used to collect money from human trafficking, and I let that go after you stopped. You've fucked prostitutes, and I let that go. You were rude to my boss, and I let that go. You've been enemies with my brother, and I let that go. But this...it's the straw that broke the camel's back."

He took a deep breath, his eyes almost closing as he processed the rejection.

"Not my father."

He closed his eyes.

I shook my head, looking at him with disgust. "Instead of wasting your time bothering me, you should be preparing for what's to come. Because my brother is coming for you —hard."

He opened his eyes. "There's nothing to prepare for. I would never hurt him."

"Whatever..."

"I would never hurt someone you love. So, if he comes after me...I don't know what I'm going to do."

"Then I suggest you leave the country and start over somewhere else. Because he's not gonna stop until you're gone."

He slid his hands into the front pockets of his jeans. "Then he's going to kill me...because I won't kill him."

THIRTEEN
HEATH

Balto stepped out of the hallway, pulling on a t-shirt as he walked. "Do you ever call?"

I helped myself to the liquor cabinet, searching for a bottle of vodka. There was none, unfortunately, so I grabbed a substitute.

"Change your codes if you don't want me to stop by unannounced." I was the only one besides the two of them who had unrestricted access to their place, because I used to occupy the third floor. And I knew he never changed it because I was family—and I was always welcome. I filled my glass then made one for him.

"None for me." He fell onto the couch.

"Then more for me." I carried both glasses to the table and sat on the other couch. The last couple weeks of my life had been filled with booze and solitude. When I went to the Underground and took care of business, I was usually out of touch with my own actions, only partially listening to conversations.

Balto watched me, his hands together on his lap as he relaxed into the couch, watching me go to town on both drinks. "What's wrong?"

"Why do you assume something's wrong?"

His eyes didn't blink. "Because you look like shit. And it's two in the morning."

"Not a night owl anymore?"

He didn't answer the question.

I downed the first drink. "One down. Another to go." I pushed the empty glass away then grabbed the other.

Balto was right on the money, and instead of interrogating me about it, he chose to hold his silence, to let me come clean when I was ready to.

I stared at the ground a long time, unsure how to handle the tightness in my chest, the devastation that had destroyed my entire body. Time and patience healed all my physical wounds, and pain could easily be treated with a couple of pills. But this...there was no shortcut for this. "She left me."

My brother didn't react. "I haven't seen you this low in a long time...so I assumed."

Was my agony that obvious?

"You told her?"

I shook my head. "Damien did."

He bowed his head slightly. "That's even worse."

"She told him about me, I think in the hope of burying our mutual grievances so she and I could be together. That just makes it so much worse, that she was willing to fight for me." I pressed my hands to my face and just sat there, imagining how that conversation backfired and exploded in her face.

"I'm sorry, Heath," he said quietly. "What are you going to do now?"

"I've tried talking to her...she wants nothing to do with me." I gave her a few weeks of space so she could calm down, let the initial flame lower to room temperature, but when I saw her at the bar, she was the same. She wasn't just hostile— but indifferent. That was the worst part, watching her burn white-hot then become an arctic winter. "All those feelings she had for me...just died."

"What kind of feelings?"

"I told her I loved her... She never said it back. But she implied it."

Now Balto's hard expression softened entirely, giving me a look he'd never shown me before. He actually felt terrible for me, actually felt the pain I felt.

"But that wasn't enough for her. She said what we had was never real...not if it was based on a lie."

He dropped his gaze and stared at the floor.

I did the same, sitting in the painful silence, wanting my brother to comfort me even though I already knew there was nothing he could do for me. "I don't know what to do."

"Heath, I don't think there is anything you can do."

I opened my eyes. "Don't say that to me."

"You know I'll never tell you what you want to hear. I'll tell you the truth. That's my job."

I raised my head and stared straight ahead. "She said she hates me, that she wishes she hadn't warned me and fucked up Damien's plan...that she wishes I were dead for what I did to her father." That hurt the most, to hear her say those things and mean every word, to wish everything we'd had never happened at all.

"You did a pretty terrible thing, Heath."

I closed my eyes in a grimace. "I was a different person then. And come on, don't make me feel worse—"

"But I find it hard to believe she really means that."

I opened my eyes and looked at him.

"Maybe she means them in the moment, but I don't think she means it literally. She doesn't strike me as the kind of person to wish death on anyone...especially the man she loves."

"*Loved*," I whispered.

He gave me another remorseful look. "I think you should give her space. A lot of it. And maybe...someday...you can try again."

"I don't want to wait until someday. I want her now."

"Well, I just don't think that's possible," he said. "This woman was in a deep and emotional relationship with you, then heard something so terrible. Of course, she feels betrayed. Of course, she feels foolish. Her mind is in shock. The initial anger is so potent that it's masked all of her other feelings. Her shell is hard, her guard is up. She's not who she used to be...because this was so traumatic for her."

God, I felt like shit.

"You have to be patient...and wait."

That meant she would sleep with other men. I'd sleep with other women. I'd have to live a numb existence until I could get her back, to finally come back to life and feel emotion once again. "I really don't want to do that."

"I know, Heath. But that's how it has to be. You knew this would happen."

"Yes," I snapped. "But I never expected..." I rubbed my hand across my chest. "I never expected it to hurt this fucking bad, to feel so goddamn lost, to feel like...I'll never be happy again." I dropped my hand.

Balto was quiet for a while, taking a deep breath like that description was painful.

"And now Damien is coming for me. I don't know what to do about that."

"Wasn't he always coming for you?"

"Yeah, but now that I hurt his sister, I know it could happen any minute. And now, I can't kill him. I can't hurt him. I can't do anything. It's like fighting with both hands pinned behind my back. He's not going to go away."

Balto sighed quietly.

"If I kill him, she really will never forgive me."

"So, no matter what, you lose."

"Yeah…" If he killed me, I'd lose Catalina forever. If I killed him, I'd lose her forever. The outcome was the same no matter what I did, unless I really did take her advice and flee the country. But I wasn't going to do that.

"You could hire someone else to do it."

I shook my head. "No."

"Then you could buy him off."

"There's no amount of money that will change his mind."

"Then give him something else he wants."

I couldn't think of anything.

"He doesn't want to pay you, right?"

"I already released him from the obligation."

"Alright, then give him his independence."

My mind started to consider the idea, to wonder if that would be enough to change his mind. "And if he said yes, then what?"

He shrugged. "Buys you some time…"

I TURNED the corner and walked down the hallway, my fingers wrapped around the green stems of the sunflowers I'd just picked hours ago. Tied with a single black ribbon, they were together in my grasp, smelling like her hair, bright like her smell.

I stopped in front of her door, feeling the connection with her grow stronger in my chest just from being near her. My eyes moved to the crack under the door, seeing the shifting blue light from the TV in the living room. She probably sat on the couch, drinking a bottle of wine by herself, skipping dinner because I wasn't there to encourage her to eat.

I closed my eyes and felt the pain worsen, felt our separation strangle me like a noose at the end of a rope. I didn't make a sound as I stood there, opening my eyes and staring at the bright yellow petals that infused the hallway with sunshine. I knew she would throw them in the trash the second she spotted them. It wouldn't make her reflect on our time together, the way we loved each other in a way that most people never got to experience. But I wanted her to know I still thought about her, that I was still here, that I still missed her...

That I still loved her.

I placed the flowers on her doorstep then pressed my palm against the door, just so I could be as close to her as possible. My forehead rested against the metal, and I stood there for a while, listening to the faint sound of the TV in the background.

I finally turned away.

Then I heard the TV turn off...and the sound of her footsteps.

Fuck, she'd heard me.

I rushed down the hallway, striding quickly without making noise. I rounded the corner just when I heard the locks turn.

There was a mirror on the wall that reflected the hallway leading to her door, so I could -watch her from my spot around the corner. She might be able to see me if she looked hard enough, but the mirror was at least twenty-five feet away, so it was unlikely.

Then I saw her.

I watched her open the door and stare down the hallway, as if she expected to see my back as I walked away. She was in her pink pajama shorts, wearing a black camisole, her hair pulled over one shoulder. There was no makeup on her face, nothing but her natural olive skin and full lips.

And she was so fucking beautiful.

So beautiful it hurt.

Coming here was a bad idea because it only made me feel worse, made me want her more.

She looked down and spotted the sunflowers. There was a slight flinch, like the sight of her favorite flowers did bring a subtle softness to her eyes because it was an involuntary reaction. She bent down and grabbed them, but she didn't bring them close to her face to smell them.

She looked annoyed, dropping her hand so flowers were held by her side.

Then she walked back into her apartment.

I SAT on the throne at the top of the platform, staring at the opposite wall without really thinking about anything. There was no reason for me to be there, but I had nowhere else to go. My house was haunted by her ghost, and I'd rather be here than listen to her old whispers, get a whiff of her scent when I opened one of my drawers or walked into my closet.

There were a few Skull Kings there, along with the girls serving beer.

No one bothered me, like they knew I didn't want to talk.

I sat with my knees apart, the diamond on my right hand. I had power, money, everything...but after losing Catalina, I felt like I'd lost everything.

Steel stepped up to me. "Heath, Damien is here."

It took me a few seconds to process what he'd said, to drop my fingers from my jaw and snap out of my haze. "Why?"

He raised both hands. "Wouldn't tell me. But he's got a lot of bags of money."

Shit, that wasn't good. "Send him in."

Steel turned to retrieve him.

Without looking at anyone in particular, I addressed the people who lingered. "Leave the room."

The guys left right away, and the girls dismissed themselves too, dropping everything they were doing so I could have the room to myself.

I stayed on my throne, waiting for him to walk in the door.

When he did, his green eyes were venomous like a snake with pointed fangs. A bag was in each hand, and he walked down the aisle between the benches and headed straight toward me. He dropped them, the heavy weight making a loud thud.

Then more men filed in, adding more bags to the pile.

I stayed in my chair, giving no reaction because this man was my enemy.

His men left, and he remained behind.

Steel stepped back into the room. "Everything has been scanned. It's just money."

All I did was slightly raise my hand from the armrest to excuse him.

Steel walked out.

Now it was just the two of us.

Damien stood at the bottom of the stairs, surrounded by the money he'd brought me. Now that he was looking me in the eye for the first time since knowing the truth about Catalina and me, he was livid, his eyes spewing fire like volcanos. His arms remained by his sides, and they shook slightly, as if seeing me in the flesh made him lose all control.

I rose from my throne and took my time walking down the stairs, knowing when I got there, I'd probably get a good punch to the face. I reached the last step and stared him down, unapologetic even though I was remorseful for everything I'd done.

He stared at me for a while before he spoke. "I'm not going to take a free pass from you—because my sister can't be bought. You'll take every euro for the next few months just as you promised."

I had no idea what to say to that. It was disappointing, that he betrayed everything he believed in because he was so enraged by what I'd done to his sister. Our situation was even worse than I anticipated.

"First, my father." He held up his forefinger. "Me." He held up another. "Annabella." A third. "Then my sister…" He held up his fourth finger before he dropped his hand. "You came into my life and fucked with everything I care about—everyone I care about." He stepped closer to me. "So, I'll stop paying you because you're dead."

I'd dismissed everyone from the room because this conversation needed to be private, so no one would know what I'd offer him. "I'm not the same person anymore, Damien." That woman had softened me, changed me, made me into a compassionate man who wanted to protect innocent people, not persecute them.

"I don't care." His lips were pressed tightly together, and his skin was stretched tight because he was so tense, so angry. "I don't care if you're the new fucking Pope. You'll pay for what you did to my family."

"I love her." I couldn't believe I'd just said that to another man besides my brother, wore my heart on my sleeve to my enemy. "I never meant to hurt her—"

"You didn't hurt her." He stepped closer. "You fucking destroyed her. She's the strongest and most fearless person I know, and now she's dead inside. She doesn't laugh. She doesn't smile. Her spunk, her passion, everything is gone." He pushed me in the chest. "Because of you."

I stepped back and didn't retaliate.

"And I'm going to kill you for that."

"Don't underestimate her," I whispered. "A woman like that doesn't let anyone defeat her."

He didn't react to the compliment, staying cold.

"I fell in love with her, Damien. And I would do anything to take it back."

That meant nothing to him.

"I'll apologize. I'll pay reparations. I'll do anything to make this right—"

"You can never make this right." He shook his head. "Unless you're dead."

"You know she loves me..."

"No, she doesn't," he said immediately. "She feels nothing—like I already said." He turned away. "I'm coming for you, Heath. You still have time to run if you want to keep breathing."

I took a deep breath, overwhelmed by the mess I'd made. "Damien."

He turned back around, his eyes sinister.

"I can give you what you want."

He stilled, unsure what that meant.

"The one thing you want more than anything—I can give it to you."

He completely turned my way, pivoting his body so his stance mirrored mine. He was either tempted by the offer or simply curious about what I had to say.

"I'll give you all of Italy. Completely your terrain. No competitors. No taxes." I offered something no one ever had, and I would pay dearly for it. I would have to shut down all my other clients, and there would definitely be backlash for it, possibly my resignation, but I had to put out this fire.

He cocked his head slightly, his eyes narrowing as he slowly took in the offer. He took a few steps toward me.

It was working. "It's yours—for a truce."

His expression didn't change, his shoulders squared. He was a strong man but on the leaner side, missing the thirty pounds of muscle that I had. He came closer to me again, his eyes cold. "No."

All my hope died.

"I can't be bought, Heath. My family is more important than all the money in the world, and I would much rather be dead than shake your hand in the form of a truce. You'll pay for what you've done to us—with your life."

FOURTEEN

CATALINA

I stared at the board and considered my next move. Now that I never threw a game, I almost always won. My father was a great player, but since he taught me everything he knew, he really stood no chance against me. I grabbed my piece and moved it.

"Something wrong, sweetheart?" He already knew what move he was going to make, so he quickly grabbed his pawn and relocated it.

"No." I stared at the board again. "Why?"

"You seem lifeless."

"Lifeless...that's a bit harsh." I examined the board as I considered how to beat him in the least number of moves.

"I've known you since you were born, sweetheart. I know when something's off."

I made my move then looked at him. "Damien told me about your kidnapping..."

"You're upset about that?" he asked incredulously. "That was like a year ago."

"Still upsets me."

"Well, everything turned out fine. My only grievance was missing my favorite show."

He was just like Damien, making a joke out of the most serious situations. "You weren't hurt?"

"No." He examined the board. "When the men came to my apartment and told me to cooperate, I listened. I know my son will move mountains for me. I never lost my faith." He made his move.

I must have been too distracted by the conversation because I moved my piece and set myself up for failure.

And he demolished me. "Checkmate."

"Damn...you got me."

"And that's how I know something is wrong." He grabbed the pieces and returned them to the start.

A slow smile spread across my lips.

Damien stepped into the dining room. "Who won?"

I nodded to my dad.

"She was distracted," Dad explained. "Hopefully, she learned her lesson."

Damien stood with his hands in his pockets, watching our father for a moment before he turned to me. "Can I talk to you for a sec?"

"Sure."

After Dad finished setting up the board, he rose from his chair. "It's time for my nap anyway..." He grabbed a few snacks off the table and took them to his room.

Damien fell into the chair across from me.

"Yes?" I propped my chin on my closed hand, resting it right on the knuckles.

He relaxed in the chair, his hands somewhere under the table. He stared at the board for a while before he looked at me. "I want your help with something."

"I'm all yours." I grabbed the first pawn and moved it.

He raised an eyebrow. "We're playing?"

"Unless you don't want your sister to kick your ass..."

He gave me a slight glare before he grabbed his piece and moved it. "It's a lot to ask, and I understand if your answer is no."

"This doesn't sound good..." I eyed the board and considered my next move. "What is it?"

"I'm gonna take down Heath, and I think you're the best way to do that."

Now, I ignored the game altogether and met his look.

"He's never alone. And when he is alone, his house is impenetrable. I need to lure him out—alone."

I didn't know how I felt about the request because I didn't feel anything at all.

"It's your chance to get retribution for what he did—and show me your loyalty."

I hadn't shown my own family loyalty at all. "What do you want me to do?"

"Is that a yes?" he asked quietly.

"Yes." I turned back to the board and moved my piece.

He was quiet for a while. "I thought you might be hesitant."

"Not at all." I raised my head and met his look. "He lied to me from the beginning. He chose to hurt me instead of doing the right thing. He chose himself over me. He's self-ish...and worthless. I don't owe him anything."

Damien gave me a look of approval. "I'm glad to hear that."

"So, what do you want me to do?"

He grabbed a piece and moved it. "I want you to ask him to come to your apartment to talk. I'll be there—and take him out."

"You're going to kill him?" I asked, my voice changing slightly.

"No."

I raised an eyebrow.

"He put you in a cage. I'm going to do the same to him."

I saw the rage in his eyes as I stared at him. "He didn't mistreat me while I was in there—"

"But he mistreated you the second he fucked you."

My eyes dropped to the board. "He may not come."

"Why wouldn't he?" he asked. "He offered to outlaw every other drug dealer in the country and give me an undisputed monopoly if I declared a truce. Trust me, if you call, he'll come."

"But he might be suspicious."

"That's fine. Won't change anything."

I considered my next move while thinking about the plan Damien had just laid out.

"Are you sure you want to do this?"

I looked at him again, thinking about my father, my brother, and myself. Heath was poison, poison that would kill us all if he wasn't dealt with. "Yes."

I STOOD at my kitchen counter and stared at the screen of my phone. Heath's name stared back at me. When'd he originally put it into my phone, I didn't know his name, so he listed it under Skull King. I'd changed it later.

I hit the button and held it to my ear.

It rang only once.

He picked up instantly, just as he'd promised. But he didn't say anything.

I was quiet, listening to the subtle sounds of movement in the background, like he was doing something in his kitchen. "Are you there?"

His deep voice came back to me instantly. "Wasn't sure if you meant to call me."

"I don't do anything unless I mean to do it." It was hard just to hear his voice, to imagine that voice ordering his men to slaughter my father while my brother had to listen over the line.

"Then how can I help you?" His voice quieted, turning restrained, like there was much more he wanted to say, but he forced himself to keep his mouth shut.

I wasn't sure if I could sound convincing when I was this angry, but I tried anyway. "I want to talk…"

He was quiet. "I'm listening."

"I want to talk in person."

"You know where to find me."

"I want you to come here."

He was quiet again, this time longer. "You always let yourself into my home whenever you want to speak to me."

"That was when we were together. We aren't together anymore, Heath. I don't have your new codes anyway."

"You do," he responded. "I never changed them."

So, I could have had Damien ambush him there. "Well, I'd rather you come here."

He didn't say anything. The silence went on so long it seemed like he'd disconnected the call. "You're setting me up."

My heart skipped a beat when he figured it out, outsmarting me without even trying. "No…" My own response wasn't believable, even to me.

"Baby, you're smart—but not smarter than the Skull King."

I looked at Damien, giving him a defeated expression. My plan had backfired, and now he knew he could never trust me. I was no longer useful.

"But I'll still come—if you give me something."

I stilled at his words, staring at my front door.

"I'll hand myself over…if you let me hold you."

I couldn't believe the request, couldn't believe he even wanted to touch me after what I'd just conspired to do.

"One minute," he whispered. "That's how long I want to hold you. Then I'll surrender—peacefully."

Why would he just give up like that? "You're tricking me."

"No. I would never trick you, baby."

"Really?" I asked sarcastically. "That's not what I remember…"

He processed the insult in silence. "I'll be there in fifteen minutes. You better uphold your end of the deal."

"You're the liar, Heath. Not me."

Click.

I dropped the phone and turned to my brother.

His expression was relaxed, like he'd heard the entire conversation from where he stood. "That was easy."

I crossed my arms over my chest and stared at the ground. "Yeah."

"You think he'll pull something?"

I wanted to say no, but I had to remind myself that I hardly knew this man, that the man I remembered wasn't who he was. "I don't know. This is the Skull King we're talking about."

"He knows I'm going to kill him. So why would he do this?"

I shrugged. "He said he would never hurt you—because of me. Maybe he thinks this is the only way."

"He could run."

I shrugged again. "I really don't know, Damien. And we won't know until he gets here."

HIS FOOTSTEPS ANNOUNCED HIS PRESENCE. His shoes made the weak floorboards creak from his heavy weight as he came closer. When he stopped altogether, the doorknob turned, as if he expected it to be unlocked without checking.

Then he came inside.

Damien stood in the living room with two of his men.

But Heath didn't look at them. He shut the door behind himself—and only stared at me.

My arms were still crossed over my chest as I leaned against the kitchen island, staring at the blue eyes that used to watch me sleep every night. It was hard not to look at him and feel that rush of anger, feel the betrayal all over again.

He looked at me for a few seconds before he came closer.

I noticed his ring was gone.

With unblinking eyes, he stared at me as he approached, his heavy shoulders squared with tension. He stopped in front of me, gazing into my eyes as if there was nothing else he wanted more, just to look at me. He knew I'd betrayed him, conspired against him, aided Damien in completing the plan I'd originally thwarted—and he didn't care.

I didn't want to touch him. I was still sick to my stomach, had been sick since Damien had told me what he did. I despised myself for being so stupid, and my usual self-confidence had vanished into a well. I'd lost a piece of myself—a piece he took. I used to think I was a smart, independent woman. Now I knew the truth—I was just a stupid girl.

His hands moved to my elbows and gently tugged them down, nudging me to open up.

I sighed and dropped my arms, wanting to swat him away.

His large arm circled the small of my back, and he gently pulled me in, directed me against his hard chest.

I felt my tits press against him the way they used to.

His other arm wrapped around me, acting like the thick bar of a cage. Both arms held me tightly as he rested his chin on the top of my head. Once we were still, he released a deep breath, his chest pressing into mine as his lungs pulled in oxygen.

I was still, my hands at my sides.

"Catalina." His deep voice commanded me, gave a wordless instruction.

I obeyed. My arms moved around his waist.

Then he squeezed me harder and held me still, his breathing so gentle, like he was about to fall asleep. He didn't move, didn't seem to care about the men who were about to take him away, as if having this quiet moment seemed to be worth whatever came next.

My face was against the top of his chest, smelling the scent that took weeks to get out of my apartment. The sheets were washed twice, the counters disinfected with bleach, his extra closed tossed down the trash chute. I'd sterilized the place so it was like he'd never been there. The flowers he left on the doorstep were shoved down the garbage disposal because I was so angry he'd ruined something so beautiful, something my father and I shared. Now I never wanted to look at a sunflower again.

When the minute passed, he whispered to me, "I love you." He released me, dropped his embrace like he'd been counting down the seconds in his head. Then he turned to my brother and the men waiting to take him away, somber in his expression. He held himself with a strong posture, but he was also docile at the same time, his arms by his sides.

Damien studied him for a few seconds, as if he expected a fight. He pulled out his gun and aimed it at him.

Heath didn't flinch, stared down the barrel of the gun as if it didn't affect him at all.

Damien nodded to the door. "After you."

Heath turned around and walked out the door. He didn't turn around to look at me once more. With his head bowed, he walked down the hallway, his arms swaying by his sides.

I crossed my arms over my chest and watched him go.

SECRET 229

Damien moved out with his two men, his gun still raised. He didn't say goodbye before he shut the door behind himself.

And then it was over.

I'd interfered with destiny when I should have kept my mouth shut. Now everything was turning out the way it was supposed to, the way it should have months ago. My heart would have been spared, so would all the humiliation.

But now it had happened...and that was all that mattered.

FIFTEEN

HEATH

I LEFT MY RING AT THE HOUSE, ALONG WITH A NOTE for Balto.

Give this to the right man.

P.S. You're still an asshole.

-Heath

He and I weren't ones for exchanging lots of words, for explaining our feelings down to the bone. He would read between the lines and know what I'd done, and by the time he read the note, I'd already be dead.

And he wouldn't retaliate...because he would understand that Catalina was still important to me.

And by extension, her brother.

I promised her I would never hurt him, and I would keep that promise.

I stepped through the double door entryway and entered his luxury home, seeing the older lady who halted when she saw me standing there, her eyes wide.

She looked terrified.

I winked. "Name's Heath."

Damien pushed me forward, shoving his palm right between my shoulder blades. "Move."

I stumbled forward, my hands tied behind my back. "Where? This place is three floors."

He stuffed his gun into the back of his jeans and grabbed me by the arm so he could escort me forward.

I didn't say it, but I could get out of this if I wanted to. His men didn't tie the rope tight enough. I could slip out of the restraints and bash his head into the wall.

But I didn't.

For once in my life...I gave up.

He took me down the hallway until we reached a large wooden door. He opened it, revealing stairs that traveled deep underground. The lights were on, so I watched my step as I moved farther underground. When I reached the bottom, I took in the sight of the large basement, which was made of concrete and had stored belongings piled in the corner. There was a large cage against the opposite wall.

I turned to him, a grin on my face. "This is starting to look like a porno, Damien."

He punched me in the face.

I staggered back, keeping my balance despite my wrists being restrained.

He opened the door and stared at me.

Now I understood he would torture me until he got tired of me. Only then would he kill me. It was disappointing because I'd hoped to have a clean death. But I still lived on the wild side, remained sarcastic, because I had nothing left to lose anymore. "It's definitely not the Marriott…"

"You put my sister in a cage." He shoved me inside and shut the door. "So, I'm going to do the same to you."

Now that I was locked behind the metal bars, I loosened the rope and tossed it on the ground.

Damien's eyes narrowed in surprise.

"Does that mean you're going to let me go, too?" I leaned against the wall and crossed my arms over my chest. "I also brought her bagels, cream cheese… But she did attack me with a plunger. Funny story…"

Damien stared at me through the bars, not the least bit amused by my jokes. "I'm going to wipe that smile off your face very soon, asshole."

———

I DIDN'T KNOW how much time had passed. There were no windows down here, so I only had the fluorescent lights for illumination. I leaned against the wall and thought about the last time I'd looked her in the eye, the last time I'd held her.

She was repulsed by me.

That made this so much easier. When I saw nothing in her gaze, I lost all hope.

Gave up.

I'd expected to die young, but in a different way. I'd expected to be murdered by my enemies, wounded in a shootout, dead on the spot with only minutes to suffer. I never expected to be thrown into a cage like an animal.

And to put myself there.

The door opened, and Damien came down the stairs. He was just in his sweatpants without a shirt, like he expected to get dirty, expected my blood to splash everywhere. He approached the cage and stared down at me.

He hadn't given me food or water.

I didn't ask for any.

He pulled out his key and unlocked the door. It creaked as it came open.

I continued to sit against the wall, staring at him with no interest. "If you think beating me and torturing me will give you satisfaction, it won't. I won't make a sound, won't beg for mercy. I'll just wait until you finally give me the sweet release of death."

"And if I don't?"

I stared at him without blinking. "I can give it to myself, if it comes to it."

Damien didn't scream at me. He didn't say anything at all. But the look on his face showed his rage, how the past still weighed heavily on his shoulders, how my relationship with his sister tore him up deep inside. The vein that ran down his forehead was fat and vibrating, and the red tint to his face showed how hard his heart was beating, how the blood was circulating everywhere. "Get your ass up."

I held up my forefinger. "Say please."

That was when he snapped and came at me, fists flying with powerful punches that seemed to come from fury, not muscle.

I took it—hit after hit.

He grabbed me by the front of the shirt and slammed his fist into my face over and over.

Until I blacked out.

BLOOD WAS on the floor of my cell. My shirt was torn clean in two.

My head throbbed like a horse had kicked me in the skull.

I opened my eyes and looked at the meal he'd left behind. A glass of water and a sandwich.

I was in so much pain I didn't even want to eat.

I rolled onto my back and groaned, my face still dripping with blood from his fist. I stared at the ceiling through swollen eyes, unsure how much time had passed, if it'd been days or just a few hours.

I felt like a pussy taking that beating, but I had no other choice. If I retaliated, I would break my promise to the one person I would always keep my promises to. My chest and ribs hurt too, like he got me there after I blacked out.

I could tolerate a lot of pain, but I hoped death was coming soon, because I didn't want to feel this way for weeks or months.

The door at the top of the stairs opened, and his footsteps sounded as he entered the basement. He reached the ground floor and slowly approached the cage. "Don't like your lunch?"

"I'm just too comfy to get up," I said sarcastically.

"Really?" He stopped at the bars of the cage. "Because you look like shit."

"I don't know, Patricia might like it."

His eyes narrowed in annoyance.

I continued to stare at the ceiling. "You can break my body, Damien. But you'll never break my spirit." I grabbed the water and drank all of it, letting it soak my dry throat. I could smash this glass into pieces, hide a shard in my pocket, and then stab him in the neck the next time he came after me. He was careless, or maybe he realized I wouldn't fight back for any reason, and that made him feel invincible. I grabbed half of the sandwich and took a bite. "Wow, if Patricia fucks as could as she cooks…"

"You just want to fuck over anyone I care about, don't you?"

I finished half of my sandwich before I turned my head slightly and looked at him. "It's a joke, Damien."

"I can read between the lines."

I turned to the ceiling again. "I didn't fuck with your sister. I loved her. Still fucking do."

He said nothing.

"Your men are idiots who don't know how to tie a knot. I could have taken you down the second we stepped inside your house. But I didn't. This glass you just brought me? I could have shattered it and hid a shard in my pocket. Sliced your neck the second you came after me. Damien, you think you have the upper hand, but the only reason you do is because I allowed it. The only reason you have me in this Ritz Carlton resort is because I allowed it. I promised Catalina I would never hurt you...and I'll keep my word, even if it claims my life."

He was quiet after he listened to my speech. "That's too bad, because you mean nothing to her."

I kept the same blank expression, but those words hurt me more than his fists ever could.

"She set you up because she wants you dead as much as I do. I've never been prouder."

I grabbed the other half of the sandwich and ate it, ignoring the unbearable pain inside my chest. It hurt because it was true. It hurt because she'd barely hugged me back, and even when she did, it didn't feel the same. It hurt because my betrayal really did change who she was. She was like a ghost, just a hazy outline of who she used to be.

Damien unlocked the door. "Do you like baseball, Heath?"

I already knew where this was going. He had a wooden bat with my name written all over it. "Just let me finish my sandwich."

SIXTEEN

CATALINA

"ARE YOU SURE YOU'RE OKAY?" ANNA SAT NEXT TO ME on the couch, her glass of wine in her slender fingers.

"Yeah. Why?" I turned to her, sipping from my glass.

"You just...seem sad."

"I'm not sad," I said defensively. "I'm not really anything."

Anna watched me for a while, like she wanted to say something but couldn't find the words. "Damien has him in the house, in the basement."

I didn't ask if he was still alive. It made no difference either way.

"Doesn't talk about it."

Probably to protect her. "He's hurt every single member of our family—including you. It's time for retribution."

"Yeah, I guess so."

A knock sounded at the door, a hard knock, like a man was on the other side.

"Expecting company?" Anna asked.

"No. It's probably Damien." I set the wine down and moved to the door. I didn't look through the peephole before I opened it, expecting to come face-to-face with the man who shared my green eyes.

But it wasn't him.

Balto stared at me on the threshold, wearing that exact same look of intensity that his brother had, expressing his unease with just his look, not needing words like most people did.

I was frozen, never expecting to see him again, never expecting to see Heath's visage looking back at me.

His chest rose and fell deeply, like he was breathing hard, either from exertion or pain.

I didn't know what to do. "Uh..."

He invited himself inside and slammed the door shut behind him.

"Oh my god..." Anna rose from the couch, probably assuming it was Heath because she didn't realize he had a twin.

Balto's eyes shifted to her. "Get the fuck out."

Anna was still, her eyes shifting to me.

"It's okay," I whispered.

Balto stared at me. "I won't hurt you...even though I'd like to." His blue eyes burned deep into mine, full of violence, revenge, and everything in between.

Anna grabbed her purse and walked out.

When the door was shut behind her, I took a step back.

But he took a step forward. "Tell me where he is."

"He's not here..."

His nostrils flared as he released an aggressive sigh. "Obviously."

I crossed my arms over my chest.

"Answer me."

"No." I shifted my gaze away, guilty for denying him when he'd been nothing but nice to me.

"Bitch." He moved closer to me. "This is my brother. My family."

"And he did terrible things to my family." I turned back to him. "He gets what he deserves."

"Deserves?" he whispered. "You'd be a slave if it weren't for him. Or did you forget that?"

When I took a breath, my lungs hurt. "No. I saved his life when he went to collect money from Damien. We're even."

"Even?" he asked. "No, you're not even. Slavery is much, much worse than death. I don't need to explain that to you." There were subtle differences between him and Heath, so insignificant no one would notice, except someone who knew them well...like me. "I understand what he did was wrong. Keeping it from you was also wrong."

"He didn't just keep it from me," I snapped. "He made me fall in love with him when he knew what was going to happen. He dragged me along—and crushed me." It was the first time I'd admitted it out loud, and it was the first time I'd felt an emotion other than rage since I confronted Heath.

Balto finally turned gentle. "I know. And he's been fairly punished if he's still alive."

I dropped my eyes.

"This isn't the answer."

"He's done terrible things to every single person in my family—"

"Before he met you. He's different now. He's a new man. I've known my brother my whole life. I've witnessed a change I didn't think was possible. I've watched him become a good man—because of you. Let the past go."

"He almost killed my father—"

"Almost," he hissed. "He's the fucking Skull King. Not Walt Disney."

I sighed as I rolled my eyes.

"But he would never do anything to you or anyone you care about again. Tell me where the fuck he is."

"It doesn't matter. You can't get inside."

His eyes narrowed. "Try me."

"He's at my brother's place. In his basement."

His eyes started to soften with disappointment, and he released a deep breath of defeat. "I was hoping he would be somewhere else. Because you're right, I can't get inside." He stepped back and turned his gaze to my living room, his hands sliding into his pockets. "Because that would require me to hurt Damien...and Heath would rather die than let that happen." He turned back to me. "Because he loves you. And I'm disappointed you've forgotten that you love him too."

IT WAS strange to be in the house.

To be in the house where Heath was either in a cage...or a corpse.

I sat across from my father and tried to play the game, but that was difficult because all I could think about was Heath's ghost.

"Sweetheart?"

I lifted my gaze to look at my father.

"It's your turn."

"I know. Just thinking."

He pulled back his sleeve to look at his watch. "I've never seen you think this long."

"Well, I want to win."

He released his sleeve and rested his elbows on the table. "I have a feeling you aren't thinking about the game."

I dropped my gaze again, not wanting to discuss my feelings. Half of me wanted Heath dead, the other half wished I were dead instead. "I don't want to talk about it, Daddy."

"Alright. But I'm always here...even if it's to talk about boys."

I looked at him again.

"Your mother died too young and isn't here to do those motherly things with you, so I can try." He shrugged. "I understand you're a grown woman who probably doesn't need help or an old man's advice, but my offer is always on the table."

His kindness made me smile. "Thanks, Daddy..." I couldn't believe Heath took this innocent man and intended to shoot him in the back of the head, just to get a few bags of cash. It made me hate him all over again, made me realize our love was never real, it was just lust and infatuation. How could I ever want to be with someone who did that to my father? What kind of future could we ever have?

Damien stepped into the dining room. "Wow, really exciting game," he said sarcastically.

"Your sister is very strategic," my father said. "Takes her time."

Damien stopped at the table, looked at the pieces for a bit, and then turned to our father. "Remember the night you were kidnapped?"

Oh my god, I didn't want to hear this.

"Yes," Dad answered. "Why?"

"I've got him in the basement. And now that I've had my fun with him, I'm going to kill him. You want to do the honors?"

There was a sudden, painful stitch in my chest, like I couldn't breathe, like my lungs wouldn't cooperate.

Dad considered the question. "That's not who I am anymore, son. I stopped doing that stuff a long time ago, atoned for my sins, because when I get to those pearly gates...I don't want to be turned away."

"You aren't killing an innocent man," Damien said. "This guy was going to kill you."

He shrugged. "But he didn't. You saved me—because love is always stronger than hate."

Damien stared him for a while, like he wanted to say something else, but then he turned to me. "Then I think you're next in line."

I couldn't pick up that gun and shoot someone, not even Heath. "No..."

He gave me a look of disappointment. "Alright. Then I'll do it." He turned around and walked out of the room.

Dad turned back to the chess game. "I see at least three moves you can make—"

"Damien." I left my chair and ran after him. I stepped into the hallway and heard him farther away, so I followed the sound of his footsteps. When I reached the wooden door, he was halfway down the steps.

He stopped and turned back to me. "Good. I'm glad you changed your mind." He descended the steps the rest of the way until he was gone from my sight. "I've got a special surprise for you. Catalina is the one who's gonna put the bullet in your brain."

Now that I'd heard those words, it all felt real. I gripped the railing and took the stairs quickly. When I reached the bottom, I was in a large concrete room, constructed generations ago before the house had been renovated.

Inside the metal cage was Heath...or what was left of him.

He lay on the ground, shirtless, bruised and bloody like he'd been ripped to pieces. He didn't even seem conscious. He was...a living corpse. "Oh my god..." I slowly moved to the cage, my eyes immediately burning with tears when I saw the blood everywhere, the stains that would permanently mark the floor of the cage forever.

Heath didn't look at me, his head turned to the other wall.

My hands gripped the bars, and I suddenly felt sick, felt weak, felt so much self-hatred that I wished I could take his place. I knew exactly how it felt to be locked in a basement, barely holding on to life, afraid of the men who kept me there. The tears were unstoppable, the pain more agonizing than anything I'd ever felt before. "Open the door." I grabbed the bars and shook them, hoping to break them loose myself.

Damien remained behind me. "What?"

I turned to him, screaming so loud I didn't even recognize myself. "*Open the fucking door!*"

Damien stilled at the ferocity that had just come out of my mouth, at the way everything around us vibrated as if an earthquake had struck the city. There was no argument from his lips, and his expression was tight, like he was actually scared of me. Wordlessly, he pulled the key from his pocket and walked to the door. Then he stepped back, staring at me like he didn't know me anymore.

I entered the cage and dropped to my knees, leaning over him as the tears burst from my eyes. "Heath." I placed my palm over his heart and felt it still beating. It was gentle and slow, like he was weak. His body had been destroyed, so bruised and swollen that I couldn't imagine how someone could take that much abuse and still be alive. My hand grabbed his chin, and I turned him to me. "Heath?"

He looked at me, but his expression was vacant, like he assumed it was a dream.

Damien finally found this voice. "Cat, I'm not letting him out of this cage. You can say goodbye—"

"He's been punished enough." I looked at him over my shoulder. "If you want to shoot him, then you better hope that bullet goes clean through me and into him."

Damien looked at me with disappointment. "Don't forget that he deserves this—"

"No one fucking deserves this." I turned back to Heath and tried to sit him up. "Get your ass over here and help me. I can't pick him up." I lowered him back to the floor because my body simply wasn't strong enough, regardless of the adrenaline.

Damien didn't move. "No."

My entire body shook with anger. I slowly turned back to him, then rose to my feet, getting in his face. "Now."

He held his hard stare.

"Love is stronger than hate, Damien. Even Dad just said so."

"You're taking that out of context. If Dad knew this was the guy you wanted to be with—"

"He would accept him with open arms—because I love him." Tears fell down my cheeks, like two rivers, dripping into my open mouth and lighting my tongue on fire with the burn of the salt. "So, you're going to help me—"

"Baby." His voice sounded the same, strong even though the rest of him was weak. "I can do it."

I turned back to him.

He rolled over onto his side, groaning as he pressed his flattened palms against the floor and started to raise himself, moving slowly because that was all he could do.

I hooked my arm under his shoulder and helped him to his feet.

He was shaky, his palm pressing against the wall for balance. He closed his eyes for an instant, grimacing through the pain.

"Damien, get his other arm."

Heath turned to the exit of the cage. "I don't need his help…" He moved forward, breathing hard as he forced his body to obey his commands.

Damien stood there, furious.

I helped Heath right past my brother, ignoring the rage on his face.

My brother didn't try to stop me.

I stopped at the stairs. "It's a long climb."

"I got it. Go in front." He gripped the railing and breathed hard.

I went first.

It took him a long time, but he pulled himself to the top, taking many breaks because his body was in awful shape.

Seeing him look so terrible killed me, ripped my heart into so many pieces, I could never put them back together.

When he reached the top, I grabbed his arm and directed him toward the entryway.

Patricia stepped out of the kitchen but halted when she saw him.

He winked at her and kept walking.

I opened the front door so he could get through. "I'll call an ambulance."

"No." He stepped into the sunlight, his injuries looking worse. "Just get me home."

"You are in no shape—"

"Call Balto." He moved down the steps to my car at the curb.

I wanted to argue, but it took him so much effort to speak that I didn't want him to waste any energy on arguing with me, force his body to endure more pain just to repeat what he'd already asked for. "Alright." I opened the door for him so he could collapse into the passenger seat, immediately closing his eyes like he couldn't do any more than that.

I got behind the wheel and pulled out my phone. "I don't have his number..."

He took the phone, dialed the number, and hit send.

I started the car and drove, the call coming through the speakerphone.

Balto answered after a few rings, sounding just like Heath. "Yes?"

"It's Catalina." I spoke through my tears, turning down the streets as I made my way to his house. "I've got Heath... He's hurt really bad. He told me to call you. I don't know what to do. He told me to drive him home—"

"I'll meet you there." He didn't ask any questions or show any sign of panic. "Pull into the garage."

I'D BARELY TURNED the engine off when Balto pulled the door open. Like one soldier picking up another, he pulled Heath's arm over his shoulder and lifted him from the seat, lifting his own body weight like it was no big deal.

I'd never seen Heath like that, and it broke my heart. He allowed someone to carry him completely, because he couldn't do it himself. It was a weakness I didn't think was possible, not after all the strength he'd shown me.

Balto carried him up the flights of stairs then down the hallway, delivering him to his bedroom.

I was close behind.

Balto gently placed him on the bed, guiding him backward until he landed softly against the mattress. "I've got meds in the car. I'll be right back."

I stood over Heath, seeing him lie there with his eyes closed, like he was already dead.

"Oh my god..." I placed my hands over my face, unable to suffer this reality, unable to deal with this cruelty.

Balto returned and dumped his bag on the dresser. Like he was a doctor who knew what he was doing, he opened bottles and dropped pills onto the counter. He even had an IV bag along with an extendable pole. "I've got our doctor on the way. But this will tide you over." He opened a bottle of water then helped him take the pills. Then he set up the IV, finding a vein and inserting it before he got the saline going. "Just give it a few minutes, you'll feel better."

Heath kept his eyes closed, lifeless.

"Fuck, is he going to be okay?" I whispered through my sobs.

Balto didn't look at me. "Yes."

"How do you know that?"

He turned to me as he rolled the pole next to his bed. "Because he has something live for."

I SAT on the couch in the living room because I didn't want to sit there and stare at Heath's broken body. I didn't want to watch the doctor examine him and describe his injuries, describe his pain.

It was too fucking much.

Balto came back into the living room.

"How is he?" I whispered.

"He's going to be asleep for a while, which is a good thing. He's got enough painkillers to keep him comfortable and to get through the night. The next few days will be rough for him, but we've got good shit for him."

My cheek was pressed into my palm, my eyes down.

"His ribs are broken, his shoulder popped out of the socket, but we popped it back in..."

I shut my eyes tight.

Balto seemed to understand how sick it made me, so he stopped with the details. "But nothing life-threatening. He'll just need some time to get back on his feet...and some help."

"I can do it." I opened my eyes again, my cheeks soaked with my tears.

He sat on the other couch, his elbows on his knees as he stared at me.

"I'll take care of him." I didn't feel obligated because it was my fault. I just wanted to do it, to make sure Heath could relax and not worry about anything as he put himself back together.

"Do I need to worry about Damien?"

I turned to him, my lungs aching. My brother was the last thing on my mind right now. "No...he let me take him away."

"Alright." He turned his head the other way, staring across the room at nothing in particular. "I'll grab some groceries so you don't need to worry about that. Are you planning to sleep here?"

I nodded.

"Want me to grab anything from your apartment?"

"Yeah...just some clothes. My makeup bag. Some pajamas."

"You got it."

"I'll give you my key—"

"I don't need it." He rose to his feet. "I'll stop by and check on him from time to time. You have my number, so call me if you need anything."

"Alright, thank you."

"I'd stay with him, but now I have work to do."

"What work?" I whispered, looking up at him.

"Heath wouldn't want his men to know what happened to him, that he's too weak to lead. So, I'll do it."

"Won't they still know he's too weak?"

He raised his right hand, where his skull ring now sat. "Not if I pretend to be him."

HEATH WAS asleep for almost an entire day, twenty-four hours straight. I had to constantly press my hand to his chest to make sure he was still breathing, he still had a heartbeat.

That night, I was too afraid to leave him alone in case he needed anything, so I slept on the couch with a pillow and blanket. I would have lain directly beside him, but I was too afraid to disturb him, to accidentally touch him and cause him pain.

The next morning, he still wasn't awake, so I went into the kitchen and made something to eat. I passed the time watching TV, going back into the room to check on him. When Balto delivered the groceries along with my belongings, he checked on him too, but he didn't make small talk before he left.

Later that night, Heath woke up.

I was sitting in the armchair and reading a book, facing his bed so I would know the second he was asleep.

He hadn't changed his position once, not since Balto had laid him down. He was practically in a coma, and he didn't look much better than he had once he'd gotten into that bed. He looked as terrible as I felt.

"Baby?" His deep voice came out as a quiet whisper, entering the room like a gentle breeze.

I dropped my book in surprise, expecting to see him stir before he actually spoke. "You're awake..." I pulled the chair up to his bed and looked down at him, careful not to touch him.

He opened his eyes and stared at me, his face different from all the swelling and bruising, his eyes almost impossible to see.

Now I understood why he couldn't look at me after he'd saved me—because it was too fucking hard. The sobs came out of nowhere, shaking my body, like a rocket going from standing still to breaking the sound barrier.

His hand moved to mine, and he interlocked our fingers. "Shh..."

I forced my sobs to stop, afraid the noise was hurting him, antagonizing a migraine.

"It may not look like it, but I've never felt better." His thumb brushed across my knuckles, moving slowly, stroking me like I was the one who needed to be comforted.

"Is there anything I can get you?"

"Yes," he whispered. "I'm starving."

"Of course." He'd been asleep a long time, and he probably didn't get much nourishment in my brother's basement. I rose to my feet and pulled my hand away. "I'll make you something good."

He grabbed my hand again, pulling me back to him.

I turned with the pull, not wanting him to exert any effort.

He stared at me for a long time, like all he wanted was to look at me, to see my eyes looking back into his. "Tell me you love me..." His fingers gripped my wrist, like he wasn't going to let me go until he got what he wanted.

I stared into his eyes as I breathed hard, felt the catharsis hit me all at once. All the anger I'd felt toward him was gone, like I'd forgiven him without actually saying the words. Now I felt every emotion with intensity, felt my extinguished fire rekindle into a blaze. The numbness was gone, and now all I could do was feel...feel everything. "I love you."

IT WAS a long week for Heath.

He spent most of his time sleeping, and if he wasn't sleeping, he wasn't talking. He didn't even want the TV on, like the battle against his pain was all he could focus on at the time. He was always eager for his medication, impatient for the next dose when the previous one wore off.

I never left the house, didn't even go to work, because I wanted to be at his side.

I made him a sandwich with a bowl of applesauce and left the plate on his nightstand. It seemed like he was asleep, and anytime he was resting, I never wanted to disturb him since he did most of his healing when he was unconscious.

But he must have heard me because he opened his eyes. He stared at me, saying nothing.

I knew Heath was in a lot of pain because he didn't make any sarcastic jokes, didn't tease me, didn't say anything at all.

That worried me most of all.

He closed his eyes again, sighing. "I really want to take a shower..." He had a binder wrapped around his ribs, stitches in places where the wound was too wide to cover with a simple bandage. He'd improved over the last week, but he was still a mess.

"You think you can stand?"

He considered the question for a long time before he answered. "Not long..."

"How about a bath?"

He smiled slightly, the first time one had covered his lips in many days. "Are you gonna give me this bath?"

"Yeah."

"Not gonna say no to that..."

"Let me get it ready." I went into the bathroom and ran the water in his enormous tub. He had a nearly empty bottle of body wash in his shower, so I dumped the rest out so I could use it to pour water over his body. Then I set a large towel on the ground so he wouldn't slip and stacked towels at the edge of the tub so his neck would be supported.

Then I returned to the bedroom. "It's ready."

He slowly got out of bed, taking it one step at a time. He let his feet rest against the rug for a moment before he stood, wincing slightly at the movement. Then he was still, testing his own strength, before he started to walk.

I held his arm as I walked him into the bathroom. I took off the binder around his ribs and then grabbed his boxers and pulled them off, ignoring his nakedness like it was inappropriate to look.

He stepped into the tub then slowly lowered himself, using the handle on the side to get into the water. The water immediately rose as his body displaced the volume, and his neck settled onto the stack of towels. He closed his eyes and sighed, like he was comfortable.

I grabbed the shampoo and squirted it into my hands before I rubbed my fingers into his hair, washing away all the oil that had collected throughout the week.

He kept his eyes closed, comfortable like he enjoyed it.

I poured the water over his head and down the back of his neck, washing away all the suds. Then I grabbed a loofah and started to rub his injured parts, cleaning his neck, his shoulders his chest.

He opened his eyes and looked at me.

I sat on the edge of the tub, rubbing the wet loofah under the water to gently clean him, barely using any pressure because his body was a nightmare of bruises, cuts, and broken bones. It was hard to look at him, and sometimes I didn't, but I couldn't do it forever, not when it would take him a long time to look normal again.

I grabbed the face wash and handed it to him.

He squirted it into his hands and gently rubbed his face, lightly tracing the swelling and bruises. Then he splashed water on his face, washing everything away. He relaxed back against the towels then watched me, his hand rising out of the water and moving to mine. He just stared at me, like that was all he wanted to do. His blue eyes weren't swollen shut anymore, so the beautiful color of his gaze was easy to see. He'd improved a bit, his face not so red and purple, but it would still be a long time before he wouldn't need painkillers anymore.

I dropped my gaze, not wanting to think about the terrible things my brother had done to him.

He squeezed my hand, silently demanding my attention.

I looked at him again, sighing in pain. "I'm so sorry..." Out of nowhere, I burst into tears. I closed my eyes as I tried to control the tears before they escaped my closed eyelids, but there were so many of them that I couldn't stop them. "Fuck, I'm sorry. I just—"

"Shh..." His palm moved to my cheek, his thumb catching some of my tears. "Baby, look at me."

I refused to open my eyes.

"Don't make me ask you again." His strong voice sounded the way it used to, like his feelings for me hadn't changed at all. Like he hadn't changed at all.

I opened my eyes again, releasing a shaky breath.

"The bruises and scars will fade. I'll defeat this—like I've defeated everything else. So, don't feel bad for me. Don't look at me like I'm weak. Because I'm still the strongest man you've ever met...and you'll see that again soon enough." His fingers slid down my face to my neck, where he squeezed me gently.

"But I did this to you..."

"*You* didn't do anything," he whispered. "Now I've paid for my sins, accepted my punishment for my crimes...and we can move on." His hand moved back to mine on the tile, his fingers interlocking with mine. "I'll be alright. I promise."

I PUT the pills on the nightstand along with a glass of water.

He propped himself on one arm, which was a lot of movement for him since he'd been lying still all week, and he popped them into his mouth and swallowed with a splash of water. He lay down again. "Where have you been sleeping?"

"The couch."

He turned to the other side of the bed and pulled down the covers. "Sleep with me."

"I don't think that's a good idea..."

"Why?" He stared up at me from his position on the bed, his head on the pillow.

"I don't want to hurt you. You know, accidentally roll onto your arm or kick you...stuff like that."

"No offense, baby. But you just don't weigh enough to inflict any damage." He patted the spot beside him. "And I'd sleep a lot better with you next to me."

I didn't want to deny him what he wanted, so I closed up the house, turned off all the lights, and then got into bed beside him. It was so nice to sleep in a bed again, the bed I used to sleep in all the time. The mattress was exactly as I remembered it, the sheets so soft. My head fell onto the soft pillow, and I turned to him, the covers pulled to my shoulder.

He stayed on his back but turned his head my way, like lying on his side was too much for him because of the injuries to his abdomen. But he reached out his hand to me, his fingers resting on mine. Then he stared at me, gazed at me with heavy eyes, like he was fighting the pain medication to stay awake, to continue to look at me. "When I saw your face, I thought I was hallucinating..."

I'd thought I was hallucinating too.

"And when I heard your voice, I thought I'd already died and gone to heaven...which didn't make sense because there's no way I'd ever make it through the gates unless I broke in. But your voice...it could only belong to an angel."

My fingers gave his a gentle squeeze.

"What changed your mind?"

There was nothing that changed my mind. Balto's words hadn't made me feel different. My father's wisdom hadn't either. "Seeing you like that..."

His eyes softened. "Yeah, I know the feeling." His eyes closed and he sighed, but he forced them open again, like he was trying to stay awake.

"Babe, go to sleep." The more rest he got, the better.

His eyes stayed closed his time, but his lips rose in a smile. "Babe...I like it when you call me that."

I STOOD in the kitchen as I made lunch, making lasagna and a Caesar salad, busting out YouTube as I tried to learn how to cook. I couldn't just keep making the same five recipes since he needed better nutrition right now.

The downstairs doors opened and closed, and then Balto came up the stairs a moment later. "Something smells good."

"Lasagna. Want to stay for dinner?"

"No. My wife cooks."

I thought it was cute he referred to Cassini as his wife, even though I'd already met her and knew her by name.

I opened the oven door and pulled out the pan before I set it on the stove.

"How is he?"

"Better."

He stopped at the kitchen counter and looked into the living room, where the TV was on for background noise.

"The past week was rough for him, just like you said it would be. But lately, he's been making jokes, smiling, being himself. It's really nice to see." I stopped at the stove, staring at the lasagna as I felt the emotion catch in my throat.

Balto turned his stare on me. "You saved him, Catalina. You could have walked out of there or pulled the trigger yourself —but you didn't."

"I know, but still..."

"Heath doesn't hold it against you...and I don't either."

"Really?" I whispered. "I expected you to hate me..." I pulled the foil off the top of the pan so the steam would rise from the melted cheese.

"No. You were there when it mattered."

I still couldn't look at him, too emotional to meet the gaze of someone I loved. Balto was the image of Heath when he was healthy, so it was hard to look at him, to see how Heath should look right now.

Balto came to my side and placed his hand on my shoulder, giving me an affectionate squeeze, a gentle embrace. Then he released me and turned away.

Heath came down the hallway, walking slower than usual, in his sweatpants and a t-shirt, wearing clothes to hide his injuries from me. "I thought I heard an asshole in my house."

Balto turned around and faced his brother. "You must be feeling better."

He took his time walking to the kitchen, his eyes on me instead of his brother. But when he came close to Balto, he directed his gaze to him.

I turned away because it was the first time I'd seen him get out of the bed and move freely, able to carry himself without being crippled by pain. I stared at the lasagna, slicing it into squares just so I had something to do to keep my face straight.

"Thanks for everything, especially the drugs. That shit does wonders."

"Yeah, I've been there." His brother clapped him on the back lightly. "I'm glad to see you on your feet again...even though your face still looks like an inflated balloon. I'm surprised Catalina has stuck around when you aren't so pretty anymore."

"That was never why she stuck around." He waggled his eyebrows before he walked over to me. "What's for dinner, baby?" He was right beside me, so he could easily see what I made, but he seemed to talk to me on purpose, to get my mind out of the dark place it'd fallen.

"Lasagna."

His arm moved around my waist, and he pressed a kiss to my temple. "Smells good." He turned to his brother. "You want to stay for dinner? There's just enough for the three of us."

"Just enough?" I asked incredulously.

"You forget how much grown men eat." Heath grabbed a glass from the cabinet and filled it with water from the refrigerator.

"Cassini already has dinner in the oven. I just came by to drop off a few things." Balto leaned against the counter and stared at his brother.

Heath turned around, mimicking his posture against the other counter.

Did they want to talk in private?

Balto crossed his arms over his chest. "Everything at the Underground is fine."

"You fooled them?" He drank from his glass, only drinking water because his usual booze was off-limits.

Balto nodded.

"Wow. I'm not sure if that's complimentary or insulting..."

"How do they not spot the difference?" I shoveled the food onto plates then added the salad. "Balto doesn't have tattoos."

"I only wear long sleeves," Balto answered. "Good thing it's cold outside."

"I think I'll be ready to get back in a couple weeks," Heath said. "I just—"

"A couple weeks?" I asked incredulously. "Try a couple months." I carried the plates to the table. "And sit down." I pulled out the chair. "You shouldn't be standing so much. You should only be resting."

Heath turned back to his brother. "Bossy, huh?"

"Cassini is bossy too."

"I guess we have the same type." He held up his glass before he walked to the chair and lowered himself onto the cushion.

"I can handle things for as long as you need." Balto came to his chair and placed his hand on his shoulder. "No rush."

Heath shook his head. "I know you hate every second of it. Cassini too."

Balto dropped his hand. "Yes. But it's temporary. And it's for you." He looked at me and nodded in goodbye before he left.

I sat across from Heath at the table. It was the first time we'd sat together for a meal since he'd been hurt because he'd had all his meals in bed.

With his elbows on the table, he got right down to business, slicing into the pasta and shoveling it into his mouth. "Damn, this is good."

I watched him eat, taking few bites because I wasn't very hungry. Our relationship felt the way it used to, like I hadn't done something terrible to him, and that left me on edge... because I didn't deserve this.

He lifted his gaze and looked at me, his cheeks still bruised, his eye sockets still purple. He had a couple cuts around his mouth, cuts from my brother's knuckles. The stubble on his jawline wasn't thick enough to hide the damage. "What is it, baby?"

I shifted the lettuce around on the plate. "I just... I don't know. Everything feels the same, when it should feel different."

"Nothing has changed. Nothing changed for me, even when we were apart." He started to eat again. "And in case you were wondering, I wasn't with anyone during those weeks." He looked at his food as he scooped bites into his mouth.

I'd never thought about it. "Me neither."

He closed his eyes for a second, releasing a deep sigh that he couldn't control. Then he continued to devour his meal.

I'd never wondered if he was with anyone or not. I was just so numb from everything that I didn't think about him at all.

But that haze had been broken when I saw him on the ground, practically dead.

"I don't blame you for anything." His voice turned quiet, no longer playful like it'd been when his brother was there.

"How can you not?" I whispered. "I set you up. Damien told me what he was going to do. It's not like I didn't know."

He dropped his fork and stared at me, his eyes turning serious. "Do you want me to be angry with you?"

"No. I just...feel terrible."

"The way I see it, you felt betrayed by what I did—and I did do it. It wasn't a victimless crime. I deserved everything that happened to me in that cell—"

"Don't say that ever again."

He closed his mouth, turning quiet.

"You didn't deserve that. Absolutely not." Tears welled in my eyes at the memory.

"It's in the past—"

"You're still all cut up and scarred...it's not in the past." Fresh tears fell down my cheeks.

He watched me for a long time, his eyes mirroring my emotion. "Well, I forgive you."

I looked at down at the table, wiping away my tears.

"Now...do you forgive me?"

I sniffled before I looked up, seeing the sincerity in his eyes.

"Do you forgive me for what I did?" he whispered. "Because if you do, I think we can move on from this...together."

I knew what he did to my father was wrong. What he did to Damien and Anna was wrong. But now that I loved him, and the love was undeniable, I couldn't stay angry about it. I couldn't live in the past. I wanted this man...regardless. "Yes. I forgive you."

———

I LAY beside him in bed, keeping space between us because he was still too injured to touch. The bruises on his face had started to fade to his normal color, the reduced swelling making his face less puffy. The discoloration around his eyes was the quickest to disappear. But he was still in bad shape.

My phone started to vibrate on the nightstand as someone called me.

I knew who it was without checking.

I reached behind me, grabbed the phone, and pressed the buttons on the side to turn it on silent without even looking. Then I dropped it back onto the wooden nightstand, the loud thump filling the bedroom.

He continued to watch me, his head slightly tilted my way. "Baby, you can't ignore him forever."

"Ignore who?" I asked, surprised he'd figured it out so easily.

"You know who."

I dropped my gaze.

"It's been a few weeks. Enough time for both of you to cool off."

"How do you know it's him?" I asked, changing the subject.

He held my gaze without blinking. "Just a hunch."

I pulled the sheet higher over my shoulder.

"Come on, you aren't scared of anything. And I promise you, he's nothing to be scared of."

I knew I had to talk to him, to have the conversation that could go in any direction. Maybe he would apologize. Or maybe he might tell me how disappointed he was. In any case, Heath was right. I had to face him...eventually.

I grabbed the phone and opened his message box.

He'd texted me a lot over the last few days.

You can't ignore me forever.

Cat, come on.

Pick up the goddamn phone.

I finally texted back. *I'll come by your place tomorrow night. We can talk then.*

Damien didn't text back, but I knew he got the message.

———

I DIDN'T STOP to say hello to my father and went straight to Damien's bedroom.

I knocked on the door, but there was no response.

I opened the door and saw him sitting there, dressed in jeans and a shirt because he'd been expecting me. He looked out the window, his arms on the armrests, a slight scowl on his face like he dreaded this conversation as much as I did.

Anna was there, and when she saw me step inside, she excused herself. "I'm going to play chess with your father." She moved past me, placing her hand on my shoulder as she went, as if she were wishing me luck.

Oh, I needed all the luck I could get.

I moved to the table and lowered myself into the chair.

He still didn't look at me, as if it was too painful to see my face.

I sat still, my heart racing a million miles a minute. My brother was someone I was always innately comfortable around, but now he felt like an enemy, felt like someone who made my hair stand on end—and not in a good way. I looked out the window for a few minutes too, just to get acclimated to the hostility before I started to speak.

I turned to him, seeing the side of his face, his hard jawline. He didn't offer me a drink. He didn't even offer me his gaze.

This conversation was going to suuuuck.

He finally turned to me, looking at me with such rage he could barely keep it inside.

I took a deep breath, hating that look.

"You haven't been home in a while. I can only assume that means one thing..."

My eyes narrowed. "He could barely walk, Damien. Yes, I've been home with him, taking care of him, because he looked like you used him as a fucking punching bag."

"Which he deserved...unless you're going to rewrite history."

I shook my head. "How can you have so much hatred inside that heart?"

"It's pretty easy," he said unapologetically. "When a man tries to kill my father, takes my future wife, lies to my sister...it comes pretty naturally. How can you have so much stupidity in your heart?"

I brushed off the insult even though it was difficult. "Damien, I love him." I said the words out loud, feeling the same pain I felt the first time I admitted it. "There's nothing I can do about that. I can't just turn it off. Trust me, I've tried. I need you to let this go. I need you to settle this feud once and for all."

He clenched his jaw like I'd just asked for a kidney.

"Not for him. But for me." I placed my hand over my heart. "You beat him to within an inch of his life. He's been punished enough. You have no idea how weak he is."

"He's not weak enough if he's not in the grave."

I dropped my hand back to the table. "Damien."

He looked out the window again.

"Look at me," I said gently, needing my brother to be himself, not this violent dictator.

He resisted for a while, like he needed a few seconds to calm himself before he turned back to me.

"I'm your sister, and I love you. I love you so much."

He sighed quietly.

"I wouldn't ask you to do this for me unless it was important to me. I never ask you for anything, Damien. You offered to buy me a house, and I said no. My love for him doesn't change my loyalty to you or Dad. I need you to drop this vendetta forever...for me."

He bowed his head, rubbing his temple like he had a migraine.

"Please..."

He closed his eyes for a few seconds.

"Heath would never hurt you, as he's proven. So, it's not even a fair fight. It's just murder."

He lifted his chin and looked at me.

"For me. Do this for me." I would get on my knees and beg if I had to. I didn't want Heath to ever be in pain again, to ever have to deal with my brother's wrath when he couldn't defend himself. "I know it's a lot to ask, but I know how much you love me too."

He raised his hand slightly to quiet me, and then he dropped it again. "Alright."

I couldn't believe he said yes. "Oh my god... Thank you." Tears welled in my eyes because I'd finally fixed everything. It would take time for us to move on from this, probably years, but it was a start. We had peace. Finally.

He crossed his arms over his chest as he slouched against the chair. "I won't come after him. I won't hurt him. I won't do anything to him."

Music to my ears.

"But I want nothing to do with him."

"Heath isn't gonna make you start paying—"

"Not what I meant," he said coldly. "You asked me to drop my vendetta. Fine. But don't expect me to like him. Don't expect me to approve of him for you. Because I don't. And Dad won't either."

"He has more of an open mind than you do—"

"Yes. He wouldn't want to kill anyone. He probably wouldn't execute Heath, despite what he did. But that doesn't mean he would want his *only* daughter to be with the guy who's responsible for so much turmoil in this family. You think he'd want his daughter to be with the fucking Skull King?" he asked incredulously. "You're living in an alternate reality if you think that's going to happen, Catalina."

All the joy left my body as my gaze dropped.

"I'm never going to shake his hand. I'll never ask about him. When we're together, I don't want you even mentioning him. You can take away my vendetta, but you can never change the way I feel about him. Now, if you love me—" he pointed to his chest "—you won't be with someone I have this much of a problem with, someone who's hurt me."

I closed my eyes, pained.

"How do you really see this working?" he asked. "You're gonna have a life with him? Completely separate for your family? Do you expect him to ask Dad's permission to marry you? And do you expect Dad to give you the answer you want to hear?"

New tears emerged, but for a different reason.

"You deserve better than him. So much better."

"So...you're just going to ostracize me from the family? I have to choose—him or my family?"

He was quiet for a long time, staring at me with a cold gaze. "I would never cut you out of my life—for any reason. You're my sister. But he'll never be welcome at Christmas, dinners, birthday parties. If you have kids with him, I'll spend time with them because they're my nieces and nephews, but I'll never spend time with their father. And you can't change the way I feel about that, Catalina."

I'd never imagined a future with Heath. My mind hadn't even entertained the idea. "Damien, I never said I was going to marry the guy—"

"Then why would you risk everything to be with him?" he countered.

I was speechless.

"Why would you have a relationship with someone that goes against everything you believe in if there wasn't an endgame?"

"I just...want to be with him. And see where it goes..."

"Well, it can never go anywhere."

I hadn't thought that far ahead. Maybe I was living in a false reality.

He leaned forward with his elbows on the table. "You can see whoever you want. You're a grown woman who can make her own decisions. If you want to be with him, I won't stop you. But you will never really be happy. Don't you see that?"

Not until now.

He continued to watch me, his eyes softening when he saw the devastated look on my face. "You're so smart. You're so beautiful. You're so damn perfect. You can have any man you want. So why want him?"

I finally forced myself out of the painful haze. "He's the only man I'll ever love…"

"I think you're too young to say something like that."

I considered telling him about the prophecy, but that seemed moot. She'd said he would always be an enemy to my family…and that was true. I could be with him for the rest of my life, but it would change my relationship with my family, pull me away from them. Heath would never be an addition to our family, always an outsider. We would be broken…forever. That wasn't what I wanted.

I wanted a husband who could bring us closer together. I wanted a husband who could be friends with my brother. I wanted a husband who would call my father Dad. I wanted…more.

I would never fall deeply in love with someone else, never have this unbelievable connection with anyone else, but was that enough to lose everything else? Lust would fade as our bodies aged.

What would we be left with?

Damien reached across the table and rested his hand on mine. "I'm not trying to hurt you. You know I would do anything to make you happy. I just want you to understand what you're signing up for. If I could feel differently about him, I would, because I would do anything for you. But...I just can't. It's not possible."

I stared at our joined hands, tears slowly dripping down my cheeks.

"I'm sorry..."

"I know you are," I whispered.

He placed his other hand on mine, surrounding my hand with both of his. Then he held it there, his head slightly bowed. "You can't choose who you love, so I know this is hard. But you also can't choose who you hate."

ALSO BY PENELOPE SKY

Order Now